GUARDIAN OF THE DARK

Bev Spencer

Cover by
Laura Fernandez

Scholastic Canada Ltd.

Scholastic Canada Ltd.
175 Hillmount Road, Markham, Ontario, Canada L6C 1Z7

Scholastic Inc.
555 Broadway, New York NY 10012, USA

Scholastic Australia Pty Limited
PO Box 579, Gosford, NSW 2250, Australia

Ashton Scholastic Ltd.
Private Bag 94407, Greenmount, Auckland, New Zealand

Scholastic Ltd.
Villiers House, Clarendon Avenue, Leamington Spa,
Warwickshire CV32 5PR, UK

Canadian Cataloguing in Publication Data
Spencer, Beverley
 Guardian of the dark

ISBN 0-590-74583-2

I. Title

PS8587.P32G82 1993   jC13'.54   C92-095362-X
PZ7.S63Gu 1993

5 4 3 2   Printed in Canada   8 9/9 0 1 2/0

Prologue

The Dragn hissed. This was the voice of death drawing ever nearer. This was the voice of doom.

The Wizard knew it only too well. Soon the Dragn would unleash all its destructive power. But it would not fly through the air to scatter fire and doom far away. No. The cataclysm would strike here, in these underground chambers. And in nearby Senedu, a city built entirely underground. Support columns would shatter. Domed roofs would crumble into rubble. Millions of tonnes of rock would smash down on the unsuspecting people, crushing bone and muscle, burying children alive. Senedu would become no more than a choked-off scream. Not one human being would survive. Perhaps the citizens of Senedu were the only people left anywhere on this world . . .

The end of mankind. Unless the Wizard could

stop the Dragn. But how? Things had changed. The Wizard could no longer command the Dragn as he once had done. The Wizard needed help, and not just any help. The wrong people could use this knowledge to do great evil. The Wizard must summon the one man whose knowledge would perfect his own, he who had the right to stand in this chamber, and he alone. All others, even if they should blunder into this place, must not be allowed to enter. The Wizard's duty was clear.

Centuries ago the Wizard could have sent his voice deep into the underground city, summoned the right man. A rock slide had made that impossible.

There was one thing he could do. The Wizard could send a simple sound — the hissing of the Dragn itself — through certain chambers. There was a pattern of echoes. If well used, it could travel far through the labyrinth of passageways and tunnels. Almost to the city itself.

Using all his remaining strength, the Wizard sent out the warning. Would anyone hear? Would anyone dare to come here, where misplaced hatred had abandoned him so long ago?

If no one came, the Wizard would be the first to die in the Dragn fire. He felt no fear as he realized this. He had been alone so long. And he was old, incredibly old — old, abandoned, useless. Death would be almost a relief.

But not for the people of Senedu — all the self-absorbed, foolish people! They must be saved. Day and night the Wizard sent the hissing of the Dragn echoing down through the tunnels toward Senedu. The warning of doom.

And he waited. Above all, the Wizard knew how to wait. But time was running out. If help did not come soon, there would be no one left alive to help.

Chapter 1

Senedu — hundreds of chambers and corridors carved long ago out of solid rock, on four levels. Senedu — all the complexity of a city: workshops, classrooms, sleeping chambers, kitchens, farming caverns, council chambers and games rooms — built entirely underground. A closed world. A city without a sun.

In Senedu it was the end of the third watch. Gen looked behind him. There was no sign of his father's servants. He had evaded them, then. For how long? the boy wondered. As much as five minims?

Gen paused at the door of a games room. He was looking for his friend, Duff. The room was a tangle of excited boys. Nearly all the other boys of Gen's age were there — playing hoop-ball or watching the game. But not Duff. Everyone was jeering, laughing and shouting. Gen couldn't resist. His dark eyes lit up. "Let me play with you!"

The words slipped out of Gen's mouth before he could prevent them. He felt the urge to kick himself. He had sworn he would never ask again!

The other boys hesitated. The game was uneven. They were missing one player. That didn't prevent them from hollering and jabbing and cheering and kicking out for the ball. Until Gen spoke. Then silence fell. Uncomfortable looks were exchanged. A few of the boys bowed their heads, as if Gen were already Guardian!

"Of course, if the son-of-the-Guardian wishes to play . . ."

"We didn't think you had time . . ."

"An honour . . ."

Someone scooped up the ball and handed it to Gen respectfully. Handed it to him! He took his place as forward wing on the red team, his lean body taut, ready to bob, weave, spin — whatever the game required. He pushed a ragged lock of black hair out of his eyes.

The game resumed. Or seemed to.

Gen should have known it would be like this — no yelling, no rude jokes, no jockeying for position. Boys parted like wooden statues, leaving Gen a clear path to the hoop. Gen dribbled through the silence and tossed the ball easily through the hoop. There was scattered applause, congratulations in deadpan voices.

"Very nice."

"Well done."

Gen turned to the others with a sick feeling in his stomach. "Stop it! I don't want any special treatment!"

Gen's voice died as he saw the carefully blank faces before him. What was the use? He couldn't make them change. Gen had spoiled the game. The boys wanted him to leave, but of course they wouldn't tell him so — not the Guardian-to-be! At least not to his face. If Duff had been here . . . but Gen couldn't rely on his one friend to change everything.

"You're right," he said in a strangled voice. "I don't have the time."

And he walked out of the games room, willing his sharply chiselled features into a neutral expression, and only half succeeding. What madness — to hope to be accepted for himself, even for a moment! Gen was the Guardian's only son. He was born to rule Senedu. The gulf between him and the other young people in Senedu had always been uncrossable. Now, only two weeks before his coming of age, it was as wide as the city.

Why couldn't Gen stop longing for the things he could never have?

And to be honest, Gen *didn't* have the time. Every morning his father's servants delivered to him a list of duties for the day, all to be completed in the scant time after classes. Lately it seemed Gen didn't have the time to breathe, let alone play games. The only games the Guardian had ever allowed Gen were the memory games — endless drills with letter and number charts that no other boy had to master. Meaningless rows of characters were no replacement for real games with other boys. Not for the first time, Gen wondered why he had to learn them at all.

"Over here, Gen!"

Gen's stiff shoulders relaxed a little as Duff hailed him from another games room.

"Can you really play now?" Duff took in Gen's flushed face, and the melee in the games room behind him. He guessed what had happened, but said nothing. Instead the redhead tossed Gen a ball.

"As long as I stay ahead of father's servants!" Gen said. "Let's get out of here. I think they're right behind me."

One day Duff had taken the empty bench beside Gen in the crowded dining hall and asked him to pass the salt. They had been friends ever since. Duff seemed to be the only person in Senedu unaffected by status and position. Without him, Gen was sure he would go mad.

They were almost through the door when someone called. "There you are, Gen!"

It was Gen's cousin, Nirrin. Gen tried not to look irritated as he faced her, but it was hard.

"How did you find me?"

A dose of his interfering cousin was more than Gen could take at the moment. His face was still red.

"I figured you couldn't resist the games rooms." Nirrin grimaced. "I'll bet you tried to play with the others. And got rejected as usual. You know those boys treat you like a disease. Give it up, Gen! You're nearly fifteen seasons old. Don't you know any better?"

"Is that what you came to tell me?" Gen's lips were tight.

"No. You were supposed to meet with Councillor Hamish twenty minims ago. Your father is furious. He's sent five servants out to find you. And two others are just around the corner."

"Including you?" Gen knew he was snapping at Nirrin but he couldn't help it. In the excitement of the game, he had completely forgotten the meeting with Hamish.

"Don't be an idiot! The Guardian doesn't know I'm here. I came to warn you! Now, think up a decent excuse and get going!"

"I figured this would happen." Duff shook his head. "Good try, Gen."

They had scarcely seen each other for dozens of watches. And now this!

Gen glared at Nirrin. "You enjoy this, don't you?"

Nirrin grinned. "Well, maybe a little."

Of all the nosy, domineering, younger relatives to have to put up with! Nirrin had an uncanny knack for knowing what Gen was up to. Come to think of it, she seemed to know everyone's business. She stopped by now and then to make Gen's life even more miserable. Or so it seemed.

At that moment, the two servants Gen thought he had evaded came into view. Gen had been out of their sight for less than ten minims. Was there anywhere in the whole of Senedu that he could go to escape his father's men? These two had been assigned to accompany Gen every day, no matter what he did. Do they hate this as much as I do? Gen asked himself. Their sour faces seemed to say yes.

"Master Gen, your father will not be pleased when he learns that you have been wasting your time again," the taller servant said severely. "The Good of Senedu demands that you attend to your duties. You are late for a meeting. Is this the discipline that the Guardian has tried to teach you?" The man's mouth was creased like a dried fruit. Gen had never seen him smile.

"No, Evan."

The other servant spoke up.

"It will be necessary to work late to make up for lost time. You must keep to your schedule! Playing is for other boys, not for the Guardian-to-be. Come with us at once. I expect we can find a suitable punishment for you."

So do I, Gen thought. With a half-hearted wave to Duff, Gen fell in beside the servants. The old, trapped feeling filled his throat so that he could hardly speak. Prisoners in detention cells had more freedom than this! At least they were allowed periods of exercise.

And no doubt Evan would tell the Guardian about Gen's ten unsupervised minims! Gen dreaded another cold rebuke from his father. Maybe the Guardian would be too busy to criticize him. He seldom had time for his son. Gen repressed a groan. Why was there time for rebukes, but never time for anything else between them? No one had ever asked Gen what *he* wanted. The Good of Senedu — that was everything! From lamp-light to lamp-dark, Gen seemed to hear of nothing else. And the Guardian cared about nothing else.

The games rooms were on Level Four. Most of the sleeping chambers were also on the lower two levels. Gen and the servants moved toward the stairs. The noise of the hoop-ball contest was left behind. The grey stone corridors ahead were almost deserted, and exactly like the featureless, sombre corridors behind. The same. Everything here was the same, watch after watch, room after room. Gen could hear the distant thud of miners' hammers in the deeper shafts. The flickering light of oil lamps cast smudged shadows as he walked.

They were halfway up the stairs to Level Three when Gen knew something was wrong. First he heard the pounding of footsteps, where there should be only quiet, then repeated crashes, guttural laughs, sneering voices. Gen ran ahead of the older men and burst into the corridor. Dark figures scattered in flight. Many oil lamps had been smashed, but enough were intact to show Gen torn garments, broken furniture and trampled shards of glass.

Vandals! Every watch now they seemed to grow bolder — rampaging through deserted corridors and destroying anything they could find. No act was too mean or petty, as long as they could vent their rage. Above the ruin, three words had been scrawled on the wall — Muck the Guardian! The scene reminded Gen of a creeping infection — a black slime that sometimes devoured the crops until they died.

"Master Gen, come back! Do not risk yourself!" Evan commanded.

Before the servants had caught up with Gen, a flame blossomed among the oil-soaked clothes. It raced through the debris. Gen grabbed a heavy dry cloak and ran to smother the flames. Smoke poured into his eyes.

"This is not suitable — " But Evan was overcome by the smoke before he could drag Gen away. The other servant stood panting.

"I can do it!" Gen called. Do this! Don't do that

— Gen was sick of being ordered around! Lashing out at the flames felt good. Coughing and choking, Gen battled the blaze. Where were the wardens when you wanted them? There just weren't enough to guard every length of corridor in the city. Before the fire was out, Gen's eyes streamed with tears from the smoke, and he was covered with soot. But the danger was past.

Now Gen would have to bathe and change before meeting with the Councillor. That would put Hamish in a fine mood! And if Gen's father saw him . . . Gen fell into step beside the servants, who were moving as quickly as they could.

Tomorrow, he thought, Duff and I will get away from all this, in the one way possible. Before I lose my mind!

He didn't see the group of Councillors walking down the corridor until he was almost upon them. It was too late to turn back. At the centre of the group was the Guardian, black hair streaked with grey, square features set in their usual stern expression. He caught sight of Gen — covered with black soot, and late.

"Father, I, I — " Gen stammered.

The Guardian stared at him in icy disapproval, and then right through him, as if his son didn't exist. Have I ever really existed for my father, Gen asked himself, except as an irritation?

"I'm sorry I'm late — "

The Guardian did not answer. Gen stumbled to a halt, his excuse trapped like a barb in his chest. The Guardian turned back to the business of running Senedu, the Councillors with him. His face flushed with shame, Gen watched his father walk away. All his life Gen had been watching his father walk away.

Chapter 2

Gen reached toward the stone ceiling of his sleeping chamber, number 53. He pried at the grating cover. It came loose under his hand. Silently, Gen levered it upward and shifted it aside, to reveal a narrow opening. He boosted himself through the gap into an air tunnel, and breathed a sigh of relief. No teacher, no servant or Council member could lecture him here. His father could not find fault with him here. And no girl cousin could see him!

The space was cramped. Gen could not stand. Yet here, in the eerie labyrinth of the air shafts, Gen felt free.

From the inside, the tunnels looked mysterious, primitive. Before and behind, dark openings in the rock snaked into the distance. Dim light seeped through the grating to reveal chips and cracks in the stone tunnel walls, the legacy of hammers wielded by men long dead — the Elders, who had built this world. "Okay, Duff," Gen whispered.

He reached down to his friend. With a smooth motion, Duff joined Gen, then helped him slip the grating back into place. Gen felt the familiar itch of curiosity, the need to learn every twist and turn in the air shafts. He turned to Duff, crouched beside him, a smear of red hair and freckles in the half-light.

"Let's go."

There was always a tingle of excitement as Gen and Duff set off in the tunnels. Gen could imagine amazing new caverns, incredible creatures, even though he knew in his heart they would never find them.

"This isn't one of your better ideas," Duff hissed. "Your dad will skin you alive if he finds out what we're up to. Me, he'll only maim a little."

Crawling around in the air tunnels was strictly forbidden. As Gen often said, "Everything worth doing is forbidden!" It only made him like the tunnels more.

"You never used to worry about that" Gen whispered.

"You never used to take off in the middle of study time."

Gen knew that Duff didn't feel the same about exploring the tunnels. Duff was completely at ease with the familiar, certain halls of Senedu.

Air shaft-crawling had been a fine, daring thing to do in their younger days, but Duff was in line for an apprenticeship as a toolmaker — one of the most respected skills in Senedu. Duff was ready to settle into the pattern expected of him. Being caught in the air shafts could change all that.

"I shouldn't have asked you to come. If they catch us you'll lose your apprenticeship." Gen hesitated. "You stay here. I'll go alone."

Duff laughed. "Sure! Think of the trouble you could get into without me! You have as much sense as a grey-wing." Attracted by the light, grey-wings often burned themselves to death in oil lamps. "No, I'm coming. But we'll have to stop this soon, you know."

"I know." There was tension in Gen's voice. A brooding look came over his angular face.

In two weeks Gen would come of age, with a ceremony sure to bore the life out of everyone under the age of twenty. He would be named Co-Guardian with his father. After that, Gen's time would be even less his own. Four servants would watch his every move and nag him about every appointment. He wouldn't be able to see Duff. Official duties would drive a permanent wedge between the friends. Gen was determined to squeeze the last bit of companionship out of the time remaining to them. Wandering the air shafts was the best possible way to spend that time.

There was something compelling about the endless maze of narrow passages carrying fresh air from room to room. Even five seasons of furtive exploration had not revealed all their secrets to the boys. Directions became confused in the darkness. It was impossible to tell what little-used storage chamber or dusty cul-de-sac lay around the next bend. This was far different from their everyday world, in which every corridor had been numbered and known from their earliest years.

"How did you get your father's servants off your back this time?" Duff asked.

"I told them we needed absolute privacy to study. We weren't to be disturbed."

Duff frowned. "I've been wondering lately. What if there's a reason for the air shafts being off limits?"

"There is a reason," Gen said. "The adults can't go there!"

The tunnels were too narrow a fit for fully grown men. The Guardian's servants could not follow Gen in.

Duff chuckled. "All right, turnip-brain. Just promise you'll turn back in thirty minims. We can't afford to be late for Truth Time again! We're still on report for the last time."

"I promise. Are you coming or aren't you?"

"Eat my dust, dirt-worm!"

Gen grinned in the dim light from the grille.

"Not that way. I'm tired of that tunnel. This way!"

Duff obligingly turned in the narrow space, twisting his skinny body around. It was more difficult to navigate the air tunnels than it used to be. The boys were getting bigger, their bony elbows and knees outgrowing the small passages before their curiosity had been exhausted. Still, Gen and Duff were adept at moving quickly in confined spaces, and they had soon left the more familiar shafts behind.

What Gen found in the dark tunnels was an illusion of freedom, not the real thing. And not just because he had to go back to classes, chores, an endless round of duties. Senedu was a closed world. The green caverns, where crops were grown under light-giving lenses, led to the kitchens and the dining chambers. The study halls led to the artisans' workshops and the meeting rooms. The sleeping chambers led to the games rooms. All of them led to the Hall of Waters — the enormous underground lake that furnished their carefully measured drinking water. None of the corridors led anywhere else. The boys might become disoriented in the air passages, but they could not really get lost. They had only to loosen a grating and drop through into a familiar chamber or corridor. Wherever they went, they would be in Senedu, their known world. Because beyond Senedu, there was nothing. The doors were sealed. There was no way out.

To Gen and Duff, the word Sky was something to be memorized for a test — a cavern larger than any other. Gen suspected sometimes that it had never existed, that it was a story the adults liked to tell. The controlled caverns of Senedu — the cool rock against Gen's hands as he crawled, the dust in his nose, the glimmer of oil lamps through the gratings as Gen and Duff slipped quietly past — these things were real and familiar. Too familiar!

The boys squeezed past a rockfall. Sharp corners of stone bit into Gen's hands. He welcomed the sensation. The corridors of Senedu had no sharp edges, no litter, no surprises. Even if the Vandals disturbed the order, the destruction they left was soon mended. Order, Balance, Rules — that was Senedu. Gen explored the uneven surfaces of the stones around him with his hands. The scent of the rocks told Gen the rockfall was old, dusty, long stabilized. Safe.

"Nothing new," Gen grunted.

"And why would we want something new? New rockfalls mean danger."

Gen didn't bother to reply. He had never been able to explain, even to Duff. Better some danger than the same stifling monotony of identical corridors, identical duties! Duff was a good friend. He treated Gen like a real person, not just a leader in training. But he didn't have Gen's burning discontent.

Then Gen's nose picked up another odour.

"Smell that?"

"Huh?"

"The Hall of Waters is that way."

They had reached one of the many branches in the passageways. Gen's sense of smell always seemed heightened in the darkness of the shafts. He could detect the presence of water just by scent. His hearing seemed unnaturally acute, too. The rasp of his clothing against the tunnel walls echoed in his ears. He stopped moving. But the echoes continued.

"That's strange."

"What?"

"Stop wiggling for a minim, Duff. Listen! I can hear something."

Sometimes the boys crawled past the muted sounds of conversation, or the clang of tools from the workshops. This sound was different. It wasn't a human voice or a hammer — more like a hiss, as if a giant creature muttered heavily in the darkness. But what creature? Nothing in Senedu spoke with such a voice. Or did it? The boys were far from any gratings now. They sat in the pitch black and strained their ears.

"What you hear is my stomach," Duff grunted. "I'm getting hungry."

"Shh! You breathe as loudly as Kargon

snores." The elderly Councillor was famous for falling asleep during meetings. But for all Gen's banter there was a catch of excitement in his voice. A new sound! Gen was almost sure of it. How long was it since he had heard or seen anything new? Since birth, it seemed.

"There!" Gen's groping hands found the opening to a new tunnel. It was higher up than usual, easy to overlook in the darkness. Without the hiss to guide him, Gen was sure he would have passed it by. "The sound is coming from that opening. We've got to see what it is!"

"We haven't been that way before, have we? This isn't a good time to try new directions. We're running out of minims."

"How can you talk about minims at a time like this? What if one of the baffles is giving out? The Council would thank us for saving the repair crew the trouble of locating it."

"You know that isn't a weak baffle!" Duff scoffed. They tended to hum rather than hiss. "A weak brain, maybe!" he muttered, shaking his head.

Gen had already moved off in the darkness.

"You're right, Duff. We haven't come this way before. Watch out, we're going up."

"Ask my opinion again sometime!"

The boys were soon climbing more than they were crawling. It was hard to find sure footing. The rock was slippery with dust. "I don't like this," Duff panted. "We must be above Level One by now. There isn't anything above Level One. Or there shouldn't be. I think we should go back, at least until after dinner."

For a second Gen was tempted to agree. But distances were hard to judge in the dark shafts. Duff must be mistaken. If this air shaft existed, it must be part of Senedu. Therefore it must be safe. Too safe, Gen almost added to himself. The voice would probably turn out to be one of the cooks crooning to his soup pot!

"Have we ever come out at a place we didn't know?" Gen said roughly. The gravel in his voice hid a longing so keen that Gen never spoke of it — a need for the unknown, the mysterious. But in the ordered halls of Senedu there was no question that did not call forth a well-worn answer. There could be no surprises. Gen half-turned in the darkness. His hand blundered against something solid. Too solid for a stink-bug, the blind white creatures that sometimes scuttled away in the passages, leaving a sour smell behind them. Cautiously Gen's hand explored the curved shape. There were also long-legs in the dark corners of Senedu, and these armoured worms could deliver a painful sting. But this wasn't a long-leg.

"Handholds! Feel around, Duff."

They had never found handholds before. The holds were regular in shape, too narrow for natural stone. And colder than the passage walls.

"Metal, Duff! They're made out of metal!"

Behind him, Duff snorted his disbelief. That was ridiculous. Metal was far too valuable to be squandered on an air shaft used by nobody but truant boys. Why, the number of rungs Gen had already counted would make any of the People rich beyond imagining!

"Must be stone," Duff muttered. "The Elders knew more about shaping stone than we do."

Gen shook his head, forgetting in his excitement that Duff couldn't see him. "The texture's wrong for stone. And the temperature. And that voice is louder! Come on."

The mystery of the rungs had only inflamed Gen's curiosity. He was climbing rapidly now. The voice had swelled until it vibrated along Gen's nerves — a vast, brooding complaint. What could make such a noise? Something enormous, something that had no name. A thing that had no name! Behind Gen in the dark, Duff rushed to keep from being left behind.

"Gen, you have as much common sense as a tangleweed!" Duff whispered. "You would chase an echo for five watches! But you know how these tunnels distort sounds."

Abruptly the passage levelled out. A large rockfall almost blocked the way, but Gen found a tortuous path through the debris. Then he realized he could see the rockfall. Dim light seeped into the passage from a grating ahead — light somehow colder, whiter than any Gen had seen before. He sprang to the grating and looked down. Silent as always whenever they came near a grating, Duff joined him.

Below them was a corridor they had never seen before.

Chapter 3

"No! Don't touch the grating! There is something wrong." Duff's voice was suddenly serious. Gen froze for an instant. The strange corridor seemed uncanny, frightening. Every corridor in Senedu was known to the boys. So how could this one be unfamiliar? It was impossible! And that hissing alien sound had grown into a word that demanded some answer . . .

"No need to rush into a sting-worm's nest! Let's think about this, Gen," said Duff, with a return of some of his humour. But just as automatically Gen moved toward the unknown. Part of him stopped breathing, afraid that the vision would vanish like a dream image. And he didn't want it to vanish. He pried open the grating. He jumped down. The hissing sound was now almost overwhelming — a summoning, but to what?

"The lamps, Duff! They don't smoke. And

where is the flame?" Parts of the ceiling glowed white, illuminating the corridor with an almost blinding light. Other parts were cracked and dull. Broken disks were set at intervals along the ceiling — decorations? But the glowing panels on the ceiling were plain. Nothing the People knew gave off light without a fire. Gen was amazed.

"Come back, Gen! We're late."

"The voice is coming from that direction . . . "

Gen started down the corridor, toward an open door, half blocked by rubble. Rubble! A tangle of objects left and not cleaned up. No sector warden would allow that.

"You promised!" Duff called.

Gen stopped. Nothing less than those words could have broken through his wonder.

"A promise is sacred between friends! Unless you wish to sever the bond . . . "

"Duff, you aren't serious! You wouldn't hold me to that —"

"I could!" Duff said grimly. "This isn't a game anymore. Think for a minim, Gen! If this isn't part of Senedu, do you know what that means?"

Gen was thinking. And his thoughts were too shocking to voice.

"There is danger here," Duff insisted. "I sense it. Turn back until we know what we're facing! Or we are friends no longer."

"Very well," Gen said tightly. "If you promise to come back here with me before first lamp-light tomorrow."

Duff hesitated. "I promise!"

It took almost more willpower than Gen had to turn his back on the alien corridor and the beckoning voice. But for the sake of Duff's friendship, he hauled himself back through the grating and they raced home.

Duff was right. They were late.

Truth Time was held in the Great Hall. Oil lamps lined the walls, illuminating the room. The Guardian faced the People. He told The Truth, as it had been told for generations — the same ceremony, season after season. Truth Time defined Senedu, as the past must always define the future. And if it were not for the past, how could The People exist?

So the Guardian led the ceremony. The People spoke the responses. They sat in orderly rows according to their assigned duties — farmers, miners, cooks, weavers, builders, those who healed with herbs, teachers, apprentices and, of course, Councillors. Duties were usually assigned for life. Every member of Senedu wore a sash by which their position could be known — green, grey, blue, black, yellow, red, white. Except children. They had not yet earned the right.

If any of the People were sick, they were carried into the hall for Truth Time on litters. Babies were brought in by their mothers. Old folks were helped in by their children. No one missed Truth Time.

..... The spirits of the Elders look kindly on us as we remember!

The voice of Gen's father carried easily over the large hall and the crowd. In his left hand the Guardian carried the Wand of Authority. It was never out of his hands. At his right stood the Dream Speaker — an old woman, now, with a worn face. Should the Guardian falter, the Dream Speaker would take up the threads of the ceremony.

..... *We remember.*

The People answered as one — old and young, one loud reverent voice.

..... In the beginning were the Elders, and they
     were wise. They lived in Sky, larger than
     many caverns.
..... *The Elders. Praise them.*
..... With their magic they walked Sky, and each
     step spanned many caverns.
..... *Praise them.*

Gen and Duff slipped into the children's rows, in front of the mining apprentices. Several adults frowned their disapproval. A look of interest flashed from one face — Gen's cousin Nirrin. Nirrin again! Gen did his best to ignore her. A single slip and Nirrin would guess everything.

Gen could not afford that, not yet. Gen wondered why Nirrin had taken the trouble to warn him yesterday. Who could say why girls did what they did? Certainly not Gen, who was far from caring. Nirrin's dark mop of hair, so like his own, fell back over her face, disguising the thoughtful look in her brown eyes. Then the boys were swallowed up in the ceremony. The Guardian went on.

..... And the People were content. For the Elders
     gave them all they needed.
..... *Praise the Elders.*
..... But then came the evil ones, the Wizards.
     They sent their Dragns to burn and plunder.
     Creatures of fire, that burned the great Sky
     place, that poisoned air and shrivelled plant.
     Curse the Wizards and their evil ways!
..... *Curse them.*

     Hands moved in a powerful curse pattern.

..... *Not of the People, the Wizards.*
     Not wise, like the Elders.
     Curse the Wizards.

     The hatred of the people was a palpable force in the hall. The Truth Time built to a crescendo of rage and awe.

..... So the Elders battled the evil Wizards,
     and cast them out. And their Dragns.
     Cast them out into their own fire.
     And they perished. So that all are gone.

A great shout went up from the People.

..... *Gone!*
..... Then the Elders fled their Sky cavern, for it
was no more.
They made Senedu. With their great magic
they made these fair caverns.
And where there was dry rock, they made
streams to flow.
And where there was barren rock, they made
green things grow.
They made all things good.
And the People were again content.
..... *Content.*

Hatred spent, the People signed their ap-
proval in blessings, woven with their hands.

..... We remember the Wizards and their evil ways.
..... *We remember.*
..... We remember the Elders and their wisdom.
..... *We shall never forget.*

Then the litany of remembrance was over.
The People sighed, shifted in their seats, began
to disperse.

As always, Gen felt an unreasoning anger
linger in his chest. Truth Time carried the People
on a tide of emotion. Gen could not think during
the ceremony. The responses were as automatic
as breathing. And as mindless. Who even knew

what the words meant anymore? The fact that Gen would someday have to stand in the place of the Guardian and lead the ceremony gave him no joy, though many he knew envied him. He stood up with a sense of discontent. What he had found today was important. It was intolerable to have to return for this — gibberish! Luckily no one could hear the blasphemy of Gen's thoughts. Wrong thinking was severely punished.

"Late again," a voice sneered behind Gen. Jered, taller than Gen and a year older, bared his crooked teeth. "Do I have to report you again?"

"No, Jered. You don't have to. You could mind your own business. That would make a refreshing change." Gen clenched his fists.

"What, and miss all the fun? One more time and you'll be up for punishment." Jered's smile widened.

"It's my report. And I'll make it myself!" Gen said angrily. He felt Duff's hand on his arm.

Gen glanced at the crowd milling around him — mothers chatting with friends, their babies on their hips, apprentices eyeing the older girls' legs, digging each other in the ribs, cooks hurrying toward the dining caverns, Councillors holding forth in small groups, their voices raised. It was a bad place to fight. Everyone would see him, and his father's rebuke would be so much the worse. Of course, Jered knew that.

"Where were you?" Jered asked. "I happen to

know you weren't in your room. I dropped by to borrow a book on nut cultivation."

"Busy," Gen replied. He didn't know what to say.

"I'm sure the Guardian would appreciate my keeping an eye on you. As a matter of fact, I think I'll volunteer for the job!"

"No need," Gen said shortly.

There was a look in Jered's eyes that Gen had seen before. There were two sicknesses in Senedu that the herbalists could not cure — the wasting sickness and the savage anger that made men lash out suddenly, unpredictably. No one knew why some of the People just withered away, and others refused to keep order, making trouble wherever they went. Like the Vandals. Jered might still adjust to his assigned duties — as a farmer's apprentice, Gen recalled, just transferred from the mining sector. But Jered's eyes seemed full of a barely controlled hatred. If he was going to cause trouble, Gen didn't want to be the target. He had better things to do.

The best reply was just to walk away. Gen pushed his way out of the crowd toward the door.

A voice beside Gen spoke. "Don't let Jered get to you. He's angry at everyone since he got transferred." It was Nirrin. "The Guardian put him on refuse collection after Barr broke his leg — you know, taking the kitchen scraps to the farming caverns to be dug into the seed beds — mud-mucking. Jered hates it. He'd rather be back in the mines with a big tough hammer in his hand."

That was all Gen needed! Jered *and* Nirrin breathing down his neck now, when there was real exploring to be done! But when he looked, his cousin had gone.

"Guardian-to-be!"

Gen turned. With a sinking feeling, he saw his father moving to intercept him. The Guardian's face was creased with displeasure. Lateness was something he hated. It went against the most sacred principles of order and discipline in Senedu. In a Guardian's son it was unforgivable.

Gen braced himself.

But Nirrin stepped to the Guardian's side, distracting him. With a grateful breath Gen slipped away. One favour to put next to all the irritating things Nirrin did!

When they were clear of the hall, Duff stopped.

"I think we should tell."

Gen pulled Duff aside. "You're crazy. What are we going to tell — that we've been going to forbidden places for five seasons? We won't be able to get an apprenticeship as a muck-digger after that!"

"You'll still become Guardian."

Gen let that pass. "Besides, we don't know what we've found yet."

"Elder magic — something only a Dream Speaker is allowed to know about. Or a Guardian."

So Duff had been thinking. The possibility had already occurred to Gen. "Nearly all the Elder magic is lost. What if we could find some of it again? Wouldn't that be worth the risk?" But neither Gen nor Duff really knew what they were risking, besides punishment and permanent disgrace. Accounts of the Elder magic were vague in the extreme.

"Gen, that's just part of it. If that hissing and that corridor are really outside Senedu — "

Duff didn't have to finish the thought. Since birth they and all the People had been taught that nothing existed outside of Senedu — no muttering creature, no gleaming halls. Nothing but solid rock. Gen met Duff's eyes. The possibility that the Guardian and the adults had been lying all these years, generation after uncounted generation, was too outrageous to contemplate.

"We have to know," Gen declared.

"Maybe it would be better not to know."

Gen shook his head quickly. "Not to know the truth?"

"We have Truth Time. That is enough."

"A set of outdated chants that we don't even understand anymore! How can you take that seriously?"

"Shh!" Duff's face blanched a little as a group of adults passed by. "Don't talk so loud! Listen, wouldn't it be better to wait until after you've come of age? You'll have authority then. People will listen to you."

"Hardly!" Gen groaned. "They'll only listen if I say the same old drivel. Besides, after that I'll never be alone. Servants and Councillors will follow me everywhere."

He could feel the responsibilities of a Co-Guardian tightening around him like a noose. His duties would double. His classes would intensify. His own apprenticeship would make the heaviest labour in the blacksmith's hall look like child's play. For the Co-Guardian must learn every task in Senedu, at least to the level of the journeyman, and in less time.

Gen didn't mind that part so much. He had already advanced far in his studies. It was the loss of privacy he dreaded. His every word, even his thoughts would be examined and corrected for years to come.

"No," Gen said grimly. "We can't wait. Whatever the mystery is, we have to solve it in the next two weeks. Or you'll have to solve it alone."

My last chance, Gen thought. This is my last chance to find adventure, to discover some unknown thing. Maybe even to uncover an immense new truth! What was the source of that siren voice? Where did that unfamiliar corridor lead?

And if Gen didn't find the truth, who would? Gen saw Duff's frown. He knew that without his own insistence, Duff would not return to the alien place.

An odd smile curled the corner of Gen's mouth. "Besides," he said, "it is the duty of the Guardian to protect the People. Maybe that voice and that place belong to some dangerous beast. I must seek out the danger, eliminate it, guard the security of Senedu, even at the cost of my own life."

The well-worn phrases rang hollow in Gen's throat. Duff did not seem to notice the twist of irony.

Gen's friend nodded unhappily. "Tomorrow, before lamp-light."

"Shh!" Gen hissed suddenly.

Behind them in the corridor Jered had appeared. Gen could only hope that he had heard nothing.

Chapter 4

Three chambers were set aside for the use of the Guardian — a sleeping chamber, an audience chamber and a small waiting room. Gen had to wait at the outer door to be admitted by the door warden, as did all the People.

The warden knocked and opened the audience chamber door, then announced, "You sent for your boy, Guardian. Here he is." Then he bowed his head respectfully and withdrew.

The Guardian did not stand to greet his son. He raised his eyes from the pile of documents beside the Wand of Authority on his large desk and frowned. At times like this the Guardian's strong features seemed to be carved from the same stone as Senedu.

"You know why I have summoned you, Gen," the Guardian said coldly.

Gen nodded.

His father's voice cracked like a whip. "Speak when you are spoken to!"

"Yes, sir."

"You, of all children, know the Rules. I will not tolerate lateness in my own son. Twice in two days! It is a fault unbecoming in any boy, but in the Guardian-to-be, it is inexcusable."

"There were reasons, sir. If you will let me explain — "

"You will offer no excuse! You will listen while I speak, and learn!

"In two weeks you become Co-Guardian. The duties you will assume allow of no tardiness, no excuses. They require complete dedication, absolute discipline! The People watch their Guardian. They judge him as harshly as you now believe I am judging you. If he fails to win their respect, their trust, he cannot guard Senedu as he should."

"But father — "

"Enough! I have instructed your sector warden. Your punishment will be severe enough to help you remember this lesson. You may go."

The Guardian touched the Wand of Authority, as if he would raise it against his own son.

Still Gen hesitated. The things he had seen today should be reported, and to the highest authority. But what could he report? A strange voice, an unknown corridor — questions that were unanswered, activities that were forbidden. Without something more, how could he make his father understand the importance of what he had seen? And if he thought his father was angry now . . . Gen looked at the closed, cold face. Why can't I talk to you? he thought. His father's command cut into his reverie.

"Go!"

Perhaps the next time he saw his father, the Guardian would be willing to listen. If Gen did nothing wrong in the meantime. And if he had something real to report.

There was a tightness in Gen's chest as he left the room. He felt it every time he saw his father. By now, he should be used to it.

If only Gen could stop disappointing the Guardian, things might be different. But there always seemed to be something. It was impossible to live up to his father's high standards.

But Gen had a duty, too. He would present a full report to his father tomorrow, after following the strange corridor to its end.

Before Gen had left the waiting room, Nirrin and her father, Arn, appeared. The man smiled warmly. He was taller than his brother the Guardian, and without the hard edges. His hair was still dark.

"Hello, Gen. Waiting to go in, or coming out?"

"Coming out."

Arn nodded. A smile touched his eyes briefly,

and then they seemed to take in Gen's rigid posture. The man said nothing. What was there to say? His hand gripped Gen's shoulder for a moment in passing. The door warden announced Councillor Arn and withdrew. Nirrin caught Gen's arm before he could leave. They were alone in the waiting room.

"Well, all your parts seem to be intact," said Nirrin. "Are you all right?"

"Yes." Gen looked at the wall. "And are you well?"

"Oh, don't put on that Guardian face with me," Nirrin said. Gen recoiled. He had been through enough today without having to put up with Nirrin's unwanted familiarity. He turned to go.

"No so fast. I'm not letting you out of here until you tell me what you're up to."

"What do you mean?"

At that moment the sound of the men's voices carried through the inner door. Eavesdropping was forbidden, of course, but the words Gen heard seemed to hold him back, like the iron grip of the head warden.

"If you could only show the boy a little affection — " That was Arn's voice.

"Affection only makes men soft. Gen cannot afford to be weak!"

"Is love a weakness, then? The need for acceptance? We all have such needs."

"A Guardian must be above all this."

"If I —"

"If you what? I tell you, Arn, as you are my brother — do not interfere with my son! Your kind of weakness could destroy him."

"Or save him."

The Guardian's voice took on a tone more menacing. "I will forbid you to see Gen if you undermine his strength! Be warned." The men lowered their voices and Gen found himself unable to meet Nirrin's eyes.

"Let's get out of here," Nirrin said.

They passed the door warden quickly, as if he could read the guilt on their faces. The short corridor was nearly deserted. "I'm sorry," Nirrin said awkwardly.

Gen tried to outdistance her, but Nirrin was as tall as he and could walk just as fast.

"Your father does love you, you know. It's just, well, he has so many worries. All of Senedu relies on him. The Council would bicker and disagree forever if he didn't make the decisions. Take today, for instance. Five different caverns want the metal found in the new mine shaft — the cooks say they can't live without new pots, the farmers say their hoes are falling to pieces, the delvers claim their chisels are impossibly brittle, the builders have run out of reinforcing rods, and the games rooms need new hoops. The Guardian has to decide what's best for Senedu."

Was there anything Nirrin didn't know? Gen stopped and turned an exasperated look on his cousin. "Did anyone ever tell you that you talk too much? And what business is it of yours anyway?"

"Just don't go doing something stupid, that's all." Nirrin's frown could be as forceful as Gen's. "Or I'll be stuck with the worst job in Senedu!"

"What job?"

"Guardian!"

Gen laughed bitterly. "You can't be Guardian. You're a girl."

"Oh, can't I? I happened to hear my father and yours talking the other night — "

"You 'happen' to hear a lot of things," said Gen. "How did it come about this time?"

"They thought I was asleep. The point is, if you don't become Guardian, I'm the only one left in the family to inherit the job."

Gen's eyes narrowed. "The People would never accept you."

"That's what you think. There was once a woman Guardian years and years ago. No one remembers, that's all." There was a sour look on Nirrin's face. "And if you think I want to give up a perfectly good apprenticeship as an herbalist because of your silly trips in the air tunnels — "

Gen gripped Nirrin's arm. "How did you know?"

"We're not all as blind as the adults! Just tell

me why. Most boys do it once to get it out of their system . . . "

"If you tell anyone, Nirrin — "

Nirrin looked disgusted. "I'd never do that."

"Well, you're always prying into my business — "

"Oh, Gen! Can't you tell the difference between prying and being interested?" Nirrin asked angrily.

"I can. But can you? This time don't interfere!"

"Interfere? I only want to help!"

"Like you helped me steal a snack from the kitchens three seasons ago, and got us both caught?"

"How can you bring that up? I was only a baby then. Come on, tell me what you and Duff found in the air shafts."

The appearance of Arn cut their argument short.

"Still bickering like brother and sister," Arn said with an indulgent smile. "You're both getting too old for that, aren't you?"

Gen gave him an uncomfortable look.

"Nirrin, you are needed at the herb beds," Arn said.

Nirrin had already gone far as an herbalist. It was said she had the gift of healing. She was certain to be apprenticed to the master herbalist if she was faithful in her duties. Nirrin gave her father a look of frustration and left.

Gen practically sighed with relief.

Arn put a hand on Gen's shoulder. "Try not to judge your father too harshly," Arn said quietly. "He does not mean to hurt you."

Gen thought that Arn was wrong — the Guardian did mean to hurt him. No man could wound so well unless he knew the effect of his words. In the art of hurting others, the Guardian was a master. But even with his uncle, whose warmth had helped to make life endurable, Gen could not explain. How often had Gen wished that Arn was his father, instead of — ? He was ashamed to admit his wish. As it was, Arn sometimes found time in his busy schedule to play hoop-ball with Gen, and that was better than nothing.

Gen was tempted to tell Arn about his discovery in the air shafts. It was better for Arn to hear it from Gen himself than from that interfering Nirrin! Not that Nirrin had a habit of telling on Gen. She wasn't usually that bad. But she was bound to attract attention to Gen when he could least afford it. Of course, Arn was on the Council, and sworn to uphold the Rules. Arn wouldn't turn Gen in, but he might try to stop him from getting into more trouble. No, Gen decided. The mystery of the air shafts had to be kept a secret until he knew what it was all about. He fervently hoped Nirrin would keep her mouth shut.

A group of Councillors appeared in the corridor and hailed Arn. "Councillor, you are late!"

"I have to go, Gen." Arn frowned with concern. "Are you all right?"

Gen nodded. "Thanks, Uncle Arn. Yes."

Gen was expected in a classroom. As he found the stairs to Level Three, he thought about Nirrin. If he could only keep her out of his business for a few more days!

On Level One, Sector Three, Nirrin weeded the herb gardens. She chewed her lip thoughtfully.

Chapter 5

Gen was dressed and waiting when Duff tapped at the air shaft grille one watch before lamplight. Gen had not slept. An extra watch scrubbing the dining hall floor had left his back stiff and his knees tender. Still, it was an easier punishment than his father's anger.

Gen winced a little as he crawled into the air shaft.

"Let's get this over with," Duff whispered.

They moved silently into the passage. Gen closed the grille behind him. The pain in his knees was soon forgotten. As quickly as stealth would allow, the boys retraced their path to the sound of the hissing voice.

What could make such a sound? Surely not a baffle, not a white-worm . . . Flitters squeaked a little as they hunted, but no distortion of sound could make a flitter hiss like this! Some mothers frightened their disobedient children with tales of a giant flitter in the nursery. Gen was long past believing in such nonsense. Real flitters were hardly bigger than his hand, and easy to kill in small spaces. They preyed on stink-bugs.

The hissing swelled as the boys neared the large rockfall. The hair rose on Gen's arms.

Gen felt a stab of uncertainty. What if the lamp-lighters had not illuminated the strange lights yet? Gen had to find out who spoke in that alien voice. But in the dark? Could he dare so much? he wondered.

"We're nearly there!"

Gen pried the grille loose, scraped a knuckle without noticing. He dropped the short distance to the smooth floor. A puff of dust rose into the air as Duff landed beside him.

"Footsteps!" Duff muttered.

"My own," Gen whispered. "See — they travel for only a few handspans and then return."

"Toward that door . . . "

Some distance ahead, fully visible in the brittle white light, rubble had half-blocked a door. Between the rubble and Gen's footprints, the dust lay smooth and untouched.

There were no People living in this corridor. Where People walked, the dust was always disturbed. No one in Senedu had come this way in many seasons. Whatever spoke, it did not walk on the floor like a man. Gen hesitated. Duff was right. There was something very wrong here.

"Gen, we must go back. We should not be here. This is not a place of the People!" Duff's voice shook.

"I have to go on, Duff. Wait for me, then."

Duff shook his head. "Stubborn fool!" he muttered. "Let's go then." They moved forward.

It was hard to talk now, hard to hear. The hissing voice filled the air, vibrated in Gen's ears. He realized that he was very much afraid.

Gen walked softly toward the door, though the relentless voice would have easily drowned out the sound of his footsteps. Carefully he stepped over the rubble which jammed the door open, and through the opening.

Above him towered the one who spoke. Gen stood frozen in horror.

It was a beast of nightmarish size. Its skin glimmered slightly in the half-light, like the scales of a fish. Its feet were hidden in a pit. Enormous wings were folded back against the massive body. The tapered head almost vanished in the heights above Gen, but he thought he could see the gleam of its eyes. Its voice filled the room with a dull thunder of discontent. "Run now!" an inner voice urged Gen. "Before it turns to see you!"

But Gen's legs had lost their strength.

A plume of breath rose from the top of the beast. Gen could not see the jaws, but he saw where the neck narrowed. The rest was hidden by distance.

At last he had a word to put to the voice, but it was not a word he wished to speak. It was a word out of legend, ceremony — Dragn. In all the tales of Senedu only the Dragn was huge beyond imagining, terrifyingly powerful, master of fire and death. Gen knew he faced a Dragn. And he knew it was alive.

Disjointed thoughts tumbled into Gen's mind — *thought it was a story, like the giant flitter. They are true, then — the bizarre tales we chant every day. I won't live to be Guardian now. That will make Nirrin sorry.*

Gen waited for the Dragn to turn and belch flames. He felt a peculiar calm. Nothing really mattered, now — not the tight place in his chest where love for his father should have been, not his hatred for the monotonous rules and duties that filled every day.

"Gen, come back!"

Gen felt Duff tug at his arm. Some of the paralysis left him. Then another voice spoke — a large, cold voice that echoed and re-echoed in the Dragn's lair.

"Who are you?"

In shock, the boys turned. Could a Dragn speak as a man? Duff dragged Gen into the corridor. They fled, skidding in the thick dust, falling in a heap of terror and bruised knees, crawling, running, gasping with more than exertion. They reached the narrow air shaft, pulled themselves, panting, into the square-edged gloom, crawled, fear at their backs, death muttering in their ears, until dry air clawed at their throats, and the sound of their own heartbeats thudded in their ears. They climbed and fell down the treacherous shafts, tearing their hands and their clothes.

Half-dead from haste and shock, they tumbled out into Gen's room — and into Jered's arms.

The older boy smiled. Beside him stood two wardens, their faces grave.

"I denounce you both for going into the forbidden place, and doing the forbidden thing!" Jered said.

With those words, Gen and Duff were taken into custody. Silently, the wardens marched them to the detention cells.

Chapter 6

The Dream Speaker threw down her handful of ancient sticks, studied the way they fell and then returned her attention to Gen's face. Her eyes were cloudy with age, and something else. The grille in the detention cell had been blocked to prevent Gen from escaping and there seemed to be scarcely enough air for Gen and his questioners. The warden waited while the Dream Speaker thought. Gen was too desperate for patience.

"You must believe me," he said again. "A special session of the Council must be called. Perhaps they will know how to save us from the Dragn."

"When did this dream first come to you, my son?" the old woman asked.

Gen could not suppress a cry of irritation. "I told you before. This was no dream! The Dragn is real! It spoke in a great hissing voice and then with words. It breathed smoke. Its great body towered over me. I was afraid and I ran."

The Dream Speaker's ancient face was creased in sympathy. She turned to the Chief Warden.

"The boy believes he speaks the truth. He has had a powerful dream."

"But I wasn't asleep! I was awake! How could I crawl around in the air shafts if I was asleep?" Gen nearly shouted the words.

The Dream Speaker nodded. "A long, dark journey . . . a confusion of the senses. It has been known before." The old woman smiled. Her face was not unkind, but it seemed to Gen to be shut tight, like a tunnel without an exit. "The boy is tired. He must rest. Punishment now would only weaken his spirit."

The Chief Warden frowned. "Yet the other boy had the same dream. How can this be?"

The Dream Speaker smiled tolerantly, as if the Chief Warden were a boy to be instructed. "The boys have been friends from their earliest years. Their dream paths overlap. Rest — that is what they need."

"I don't need rest," Gen fairly screamed. "I need someone to listen to me!" With an effort he brought himself under control. "There is great danger to Senedu, Chief Warden. I know I did forbidden things, but surely the Dragn is what matters now. Someone must go there and slay it, or it will destroy us all!"

Doubt entered the craggy face of the Chief Warden. But before he could say anything, the Dream Speaker began to chant.

"So the Elders battled the evil Wizards, and cast them out. And their Dragns. Cast them out into their own fire. And they perished. So that all are gone!

"Gone, Guardian-to-be! The Elders cast out all Dragns, with the Wizards, their masters, into fire."

"Out where?" Gen cried. "Into another cavern? Into a hall like the Hall of Waters? Perhaps they didn't all die. Perhaps they only slept, and healed their wounds! What did they look like? We have no pictures of Dragns. Books speaking of them are forbidden, except to you and the Guardian. Tell me this. Am I right? Were they tall, with vast wings?"

The Dream Speaker's face paled. Her lips formed a tight white line.

Gen wasn't finished. "Did the Dragns' bodies rise to great heights and narrow to a small head? Did they breathe smoke? And if I'm right, how do I know these things, unless I really saw one?"

The Dream Speaker rose stiffly to her feet. With her crooked fingers she cast a barrier of charms between her and Gen's rash words. "I forgive you your wrong thinking because of the dream-fever! But I am not required to stay and listen to it! Take care, son-of-the-Guardian. The People will accept no madman as their leader!"

She swept her sticks into a worn pouch and stood imperiously by the cell door, waiting for the Warden to unlock it. He carefully locked the door again after they had left.

"At least call my father," Gen cried to her retreating back. "Tell him what I said."

The old woman seemed to pause halfway down the outer corridor. But she did not turn back. Might as well ask a stone for mercy, Gen thought. Then she answered. "The Dragns could not speak! Another proof that you merely dreamed!" Then she had gone. The Chief Warden followed her.

Another door clanged shut behind them.

But the Dragn *had* spoken! Gen had heard it. Gen found himself alone, arguing with himself.

He knew he had gone too far. He had said unthinkable things, and in the presence of important adults. He didn't care. Someone had to listen to him! Someone had to believe! Here, in Senedu, death waited to strike.

No, not in Senedu. Somewhere in the air shafts Gen and Duff had passed a barrier, passed it without knowing in the dark. The Dragn was not in Senedu. But it was close. Too close.

For the first time the stone walls of Senedu seemed fragile, as fragile as frost flowers in the cold caverns. One touch and they would crumble. If Dragns could destroy the strong fortresses of the Elders, the doors of Senedu would be scant protection. And the People would die in Dragn fire.

Gen had to save them. But how? It was forbidden to speak of the Dragns except in ceremony. So many things were forbidden! In the small, airless cell Gen nearly laughed aloud. He was locked in a detention cell. His father would not even come to see him, and he would save Senedu!

Maybe he *was* dreaming.

His mind returned to the nagging thought of his friend, Duff. Gen was responsible for getting Duff into this trouble. They had been separated after their arrest and Gen had no idea where his friend had been taken. He hoped that Duff was all right. At least Duff would speak with more care than Gen had done.

Gen needed to talk to Duff. He needed help figuring this out.

A voice jolted Gen out of his thoughts.

"How does it feel?" someone at the cell door drawled.

"Jered!"

"I figure you'll be on muck duty for the rest of your life, like me. How does it feel? You and your father are used to giving orders, not taking them." Jered's voice was rough. "Moving people around without a word of apology! Ruining lives with a single word! My old friends haven't the time of day for a muck collector. But what do you care?"

Gen sprang to his feet. "Where's Duff?"

Jered's face took on an uncomfortable expression. "Five cells down. Don't worry. He's all right, except you've ruined his life, too."

"Where are the wardens? Can they hear us?"

Jered shook his head. "I'm a hero around here just now. They're down the way. Not that this will get me back my old job. I didn't expect that. But maybe you have an idea how it feels now!"

Gen frowned. It was hard to work out what Jered meant. Gen was too worried to listen closely. Was he apologizing?

"That doesn't matter now."

Jered looked disgusted. "Of course not. The little people never matter."

Jered was hardly little. He was a head taller than Gen and his entire frame was broader. But Gen knew that wasn't what Jered meant. He meant the ordinary people, not related to the Guardian.

"Just listen. We don't have much time. The whole of Senedu is in great danger, but no one will believe me!"

Jered's torrent of words was checked in midstream. He seemed to really look at Gen for the first time.

Gen went on to describe what he and Duff had seen.

Jered's eyes narrowed. "If this is your way of getting even, telling me wild tales. . . . You're trying to scare me to death! Or have me arrested for wrong thinking!"

"No!" Gen cried. "You used to work in the mines. Everyone knows how much courage that takes! I just want you to believe me."

"Why me?"

Gen cursed. "What choice have I got? Do you see any other visitors? Get word to my father. Tell him exactly what I told you. Maybe he can do something to save us all! I don't understand why he hasn't come to see me."

Something of Gen's desperation seemed to penetrate Jered's calm. He glanced around to make sure no one was in sight.

"Don't you know what happens to people who go around telling false tales, blasphemous tales?" Jered hissed. "People who are caught for wrong thinking?"

Gen nodded. "They're un-named."

"Right. I'm doomed to dig in the muck for the rest of my days, and now you want to fix it so no one will ever speak to me again! Do you think I'm crazed?"

"It's not that, believe me!"

"Sure, and I'm the Guardian!"

"I wish you were," Gen groaned under his breath.

"What did you say?"

"I wish you were my father," Gen snapped. "Then I'd tell you, and you wouldn't be afraid to do something about it."

Another mistake, Gen thought — trying to talk to a dirt-pusher like Jered. If only Jered hadn't turned him in, Gen could have gotten to his father with his warning. This was all Jered's fault.

No. Even if Gen had spoken to his father, the end might have been the same. In all honesty, did Gen imagine that the Guardian would believe his bizarre story? His father's iron face formed in his mind. He shook his head wearily. Some things had to be seen to be believed. Jered was staring at Gen as if he were a stink-bug. The older boy turned to go.

"Wait!" Gen cried. He had another idea. "If you don't want to speak to the Guardian, get word to my Uncle Arn. He'll understand. I promise!"

Jered seemed to be too angry to speak. He walked away without a word. Gen was left alone.

Gen tried for many minims to get Duff's attention without attracting the wardens' anger. It didn't work. Duff's cell was too far away. He couldn't hear Gen's calls.

Time in the cell took on the quality of a nightmare. Gen paced until he was exhausted. A meal of thin soy gruel was delivered by a severe-faced guard. The oil lamps were trimmed for the last watch. Guards relieved the wardens and wished them good rest. Gen threw himself on his hard pallet. Sleep would not come. A giant shape, a shape of menace and fear hissed in his ears, lurked behind his eyelids. Death comes, Gen thought. And I can't do anything about it.

Chapter 7

A soft scraping noise awakened Gen. In the dim light of the lamp he saw his cell door swing open. Something crawled through the opening and groped for Gen's arm. Gen stifled a cry.

"Shh!"

"Jered! What are you doing here?"

"Ruining my life. Shut up. Give me a boost." Jered turned swiftly and closed the cell door.

"I thought you didn't believe me," Gen said.

"Did I say I believed you now? I'll tell you one thing — I'm not blaspheming to the Guardian himself or to Councillor Arn without some proof. We haven't got much time. I asked for a boost."

Gen bent over obediently. Jered stood on his back. There was a low rasp as Jered forced a forge-hardened wedge into the grille cover. He pried it loose, opening the way to the air shaft. Then he jumped down.

"Where are we going?"

"You're going to show me your Dragn. If it's real, I talk to your father. If not, I make the rest of your life a misery."

"Fine."

Gen's eyes met Jered's in the gloom.

"All right. Let's go."

"What about Duff?"

"He stays here. Then you've got a good reason to come back."

"Of course I'm coming back," scoffed Gen. "Where are the wardens?"

"I put sleepweed in their soup."

Gen nearly choked. "They'll find out who did it! When they wake up with blinding headaches they'll know. At watch-end — "

"By that time we'll be back. You'll be locked up, and I'll be gone."

Even then, Gen knew the plan was risky. The dosage of sleepweed had to be precisely calculated. Too little, and the guards would wake up before they were back. Too much, and they would die. Gen looked at Jered with a kind of amazement.

"Besides, if you're right, none of this will matter," Jered said softly.

"And if we don't come back?"

"There's a letter under my blankets. It's addressed to Councillor Arn."

Gen found himself smiling. "That was smart."

"I suppose you think you have to be born in a Guardian's chamber to have brains!" Jered snapped.

Gen hoisted himself from the pallet to the air shaft. "Shouldn't we take a lamp?" Jered called.

"Too hard to carry. We feel our way in the dark."

"Oh."

There were grunting sounds as Jered lifted his heavier body into the narrow shaft. They didn't bother to replace the grating. If the wardens woke up, there would be no hiding Gen's escape.

Jered was too big to move silently through the cramped ventilation tunnels. It seemed to Gen as if the whole of Senedu could hear them. But he knew the rustle of Jered's clothing, the thump of his knees was magnified by the small space. In reality, no one would know they had gone, if they were careful. And if they got back in time. Soon they were crawling over the jagged stones at the first rockfall.

"The smell," Gen hissed.

"What about it?"

"It's changed. These rocks — here, and here. They have fallen recently. Since yesterday."

Gen didn't like that. It meant that the passageways were becoming increasingly unstable. There was always the chance of being trapped in a rockfall. Until now, Gen had thought the possibility remote.

"These passageways weren't constructed to take the strain of people crawling around in them every minim. There are no support trusses or reinforced arches," Jered grunted.

Gen had never thought of that. Of course, he hadn't trained as a miner. Not yet.

"Any fool would know that," Jered snapped.

Gen felt himself colouring in the dark. "Let's move on quickly, then." Gen was thinking of the rock-filled area in the new passage. If this small fault was worse. . . .

It took longer than Gen had anticipated to move through the tunnels. He had taken for granted the ease of long practice. Jered moved awkwardly in the small space. Gen felt more and more uneasy. It was impossible to hurry.

At last they were close to the vertical shaft. The hissing of the Dragn vibrated in the passages.

"Air rushing through the tunnels. It doesn't mean anything," Jered said.

He was panting behind Gen now. His voice held a crackle of irritation.

"Don't these tunnels get any bigger?"

Jered climbed the handholds without comment. He seemed to have run out of patience.

They came to the large rockfall. Gen sighed with relief. A few boulders had fallen, but there was still room to squeeze through.

But Gen had not counted on one thing.

He wriggled through the rockfall. Then he heard Jered swear.

"You expect me to get through that?"

"I did."

"You could squeeze through a keyhole, you're so skinny. I'm not a kid anymore."

"We can move the stones."

"Without tools? Some of these must weigh more than a man. I have to admit, you had me going for a while. But this sort of trick . . . "

"It's no trick. I give you my pledge!"

"Your pledge!" The bark of Jered's laugh sounded harsh in the dark. "The word of a Guardian-to-be, who can twist the laws and the lives of people any way he wishes! What is that worth? The Good of Senedu — that's your excuse for doing anything you want! I was a good miner! I didn't deserve the worst job in Senedu. Miners are respected! But a mud-mucker!" The disgust in Jered's voice grated on Gen's nerves. "That wasn't enough for you, was it? You lied to bring me even lower. I'll never let you forget it! Now I'm going back. Ouch! How do you turn around in here? To think what I risked for you!"

Gen worked his way back through the rockfall, to help Jered. "You can't go yet," he cried. "You haven't seen the Dragn!"

"And I'm not going to see it, am I? Because it doesn't exist!" Jered shouted.

His shout reverberated like thunder through

the narrow passage. Was that a rumble following the thunder? Or was it Gen's imagination?

Chapter 8

When Nirrin got to the detention cells she saw the wardens sprawled in sleep. She smelled sleepweed on their breath.

Rapidly she checked the men. They would recover, but not for many minims.

Too late! she thought, and raced to the cells.

It was true. Gen had gone.

Nirrin had guessed that Gen might do something stupid tonight — something else stupid, that is. He had already compromised his chances of becoming Guardian. If Nirrin hadn't fallen asleep waiting for her father to go to bed, this wouldn't have happened.

How had Gen gotten away? He must have had outside help. Jered had been hanging around the cells all day, but would he help Gen? He was pretty angry about being transferred. And he had turned Gen in to begin with!

Nirrin bit her lip, unsure what to do next. If Gen didn't get back before the wardens woke up, he would be in really serious trouble. Nirrin assumed he had gone back into the air shafts — the grille had been forced open. She couldn't follow him there. She didn't know the way. But she ought to warn him. She ran first to Duff's cell. Would he still be there? A whisper interrupted her thoughts. "Nirrin!"

"Duff?"

This was strange. Gen had left Duff behind.

"Tell me what's going on," Duff asked. "Jered went toward Gen's cell last watch and he never came back. Not that I wanted him to come back . . ."

"Gen must have taken him into the air tunnels," Nirrin said. "Though why he should take that tale-telling —"

"That bean-brain! Gen can't leave a mystery alone, even when it's dangerous. He shouldn't have gone back in there!"

"Maybe not, but he did. And apparently with Jered." Nirrin shook her head. She couldn't understand it. There was only one thing to do. "We'd better go after them."

"Oh no! Don't you have any more sense than your cousin?"

"If Gen gets caught again he's going to be un-named, outcast. I heard my father talking with the Guardian. Actually, they were arguing."

"The Guardian wouldn't! He couldn't cast out his own son!"

Nirrin's voice was grim. "He could."

An outcast became invisible in Senedu. No one could speak to him, listen to his words, or give him work. He had no name. He did not exist. An outcast had to steal his food from the kitchen, because no one would serve him. Outcasts seldom lived long. They died, it was said, from loneliness. Nirrin knew the Guardian was harsh, but this — "I think he's trying to hide something. Come on. Tell me what you found in the tunnels."

"A Dragn!"

Nirrin gasped. "Tell me everything."

Before Duff had finished, Nirrin cut in. "Wait here. We're going after Gen. I'll be right back."

Since Duff was still locked in a detention cell, he had little choice but to wait. He paced his cell. "A dirt-worm has more sense," he muttered.

In a few minims Nirrin returned. She had the keys to the cells. She and Duff raced to the open air shaft in Gen's cell. "We have two watches left before the lamp-lighters discover the wardens have been given a potion," said Nirrin.

"We'd better hurry," Duff said.

"You know the way to this Dragn. You lead. Disgusting places, air shafts," Nirrin muttered.

She followed Duff into the tunnels.

Chapter 9

Gen swallowed his angry retort. Here they were, almost at the Dragn's lair, within sound of the great beast's voice, and Jered wanted to turn back. Without seeing proof that the Dragn really existed! Had they come all this way for nothing? Gen half-turned in the air shaft, but of course it was too dark to see Jered behind him. Jered couldn't fit through the large rockfall. Another way had to be found. Why didn't Jered just back up in the tunnel instead of arguing? Shouting wasn't going to solve anything, and it might even be dangerous in these old air shafts. Gen kept his voice low and steady.

"Please keep your voice down, Jered. Did you hear that rumble? These tunnels may be unstable. Noise or sudden movement could start —"

"Stop giving me the runaround!" Jered snapped. "I've had enough of your tricks. You've lied about this monster. I'm going back."

"Not yet! There was a side tunnel not far back. I think I can follow the Dragn's voice from there. If you swear that you've seen the Dragn, maybe the Council will believe it. Then you can get word to my father. Give me another chance!"

"Why should I?" Jered grunted as his shoulders came up hard against an unseen outcropping of stone. "I'm only a mud-mucker!"

Gen's patience gave way. "I'd rather be a mud-mucker than the Guardian-to-be. Even the lowliest farmers can joke with their friends, play in the gaming rooms, sit in the company of their fellows. Not me! Nearly everyone treats me like a disease. And you talk about the Good of Senedu! That's all I hear from morning to night!"

"You string a good line!"

"Let me prove it to you. Your anger or mine — what do they matter if there really is a Dragn at the end of these tunnels? I tell you, that hissing is the Dragn itself! Now crawl further back in the tunnel, so we can find a different route."

Nothing but the Dragn's voice answered Gen at first. That dreadful summons, that terrifying word. Jered couldn't give up now! The fate of all Senedu was in his hands! At last he heard Jered grunt, "So, the Guardian-to-be thinks himself hard done by! Who would have thought it? All right. We'll try once more. Give me a minim.

I think I can turn around if I just ease past this — "

Jered's voice was cut off by a louder rumble.

"Be careful!" Gen cried. "Don't — "

The rumble turned to a roar. Rock gave way and fell with a crash into the tunnel. Clouds of dust surged into Gen's face, choking him. He doubled up, coughing.

"Jered! Jered, are you all right? Answer me!"

In the stifling darkness, Gen couldn't see the other boy. At first Gen could hear only the maddening hiss of the Dragn. It overwhelmed thought, it mocked the petty lives and deaths of boys. If Jered had been crushed . . . Then Gen heard a racking cough behind him. At least Jered was alive!

"Are you hurt?" Gen called.

"No. A few cuts, maybe. Chips of flying stone — "

"Don't try to turn around again. And don't shout! This part of the tunnels is too unstable. Just work your way back, feet first."

"All right."

Gen drew a ragged breath. They were unharmed. Gen would not have forgiven himself if Jered had been hurt. Bit by bit, they retraced their path. Gen was close to Jered now. The scent of fear was in the tunnel.

"Stop," Jered rasped.

"No, don't stop now. We have to get clear of this unstable area."

"I have to stop!"

Something about Jered's voice sent a chill into Gen.

"What is it?"

"There's a new rockfall behind me. I can't get past it." A lump seemed to form in Gen's belly.

"Feel around the stones for a gap."

"I — I can't get my hands down there. The tunnel is too narrow."

"Then feel with your feet. Take off your shoes." Gen tried to keep his voice calm.

Squirming sounds filled the black space. Jered grunted. "No use! The tunnel is completely blocked behind me!" An edge of desperation was creeping into Jered's voice.

Gen couldn't slip past Jered. The older boy was as much a barrier in the narrow space as the rockfall itself. Gen would have to go ahead, circle back, free Jered from the other side . . . "I'll work my way around you in the other tunnels, and clear the rockfall," Gen said. "I'll find something to use as a brace. Wait here. I'll be back soon."

"Sure," Jered said, his voice suddenly quiet.

Gen raced ahead in the tunnel. He came to the old rockfall. Here, too, the smell of newly fallen rocks was everywhere. It had been a tight fit before. . . . Biting back his fears, Gen started to wiggle through the boulders. His hands felt ahead and met a wall of rock where there had been a narrow passage before. Gen tried to shift one stone, gently. Above him, the stones groaned. The whole section of tunnel was loose now, ready to give way. It shifted!

Gen tore back through the passage, heedless of scrapes and cuts. A low rattle. A thud. The passage was truly blocked now. Try to move any of these stones and the whole tunnel roof would collapse.

Gen's heart pounded in his ears.

They were trapped, unable to move forward or back. There were no side tunnels in this section, no grilles.

There was no way out.

Carefully Gen felt his way back to the open section of tunnel where Jered lay.

"Jered — "

"Couldn't get through, could you?"

"No."

Jered swore.

"I'm sorry. I didn't know this journey would be so dangerous," Gen said.

"Yeah, sure."

Silence filled the cramped, dark air between them. A silence complete except for that monstrous, hissing voice.

"They'll come after us, won't they?" Jered asked. "One farmer more or less, who cares? But they wouldn't let the Guardian-to-be die in the air shafts. They'll discover you're gone and come after us."

Gen didn't reply. What would the Guardian do? My father, Gen corrected himself. What will my father do when I don't come back? Gen could not find an answer.

"Duff will come," Gen said, with a sudden feeling of relief. He knew he could depend on his friend.

"Duff is locked up!" Jered rasped. "He's not about to go anywhere."

With a sinking feeling, Gen realized Jered was right.

Chapter 10

Nirrin had just put her hand on an unwary stink-bug in the dark and she was not in a good mood. It had sprayed its noxious fumes almost in her face. Anyway, she hated the closed, narrow feeling of cramped spaces. She felt miserable. And Gen would probably only insult her when they finally found him. "Ugh! Aren't we there yet, Duff? I feel like I've been in these horrible tunnels for half my life."

"Shh!"

There was no way of knowing whether they were near a grille during sleep time, since so many chambers were darkened. If they were caught now. . . .

"No, we're not there yet," Duff whispered. He sounded unhappy.

"Well, we've got to hurry! We've all got to get back to the cells before lamp-light. How much further?"

There was an uncomfortable pause.

"I don't know."

"You don't — "

"I'm sorry, Nirrin. I'm lost."

"Lost!" If Nirrin could have found Duff in the dark, she would have throttled him. "How can we be lost?"

"The detention cells aren't part of our regular route! I've never tried to find the way from there before."

Nirrin stifled her next comment.

"I'm sure we've climbed high enough," Duff said firmly. "And we've come in the right general direction, but . . . "

"We'll just have to climb through the next grille we find to get our bearings."

"Yes," Duff agreed. "We'll have to risk it."

"I hope we don't land on the Guardian's bed," Nirrin said. Duff didn't bother to reply.

It was pitch black in the tunnels. Dust threatened to make Nirrin sneeze, and the smell of the stink-bug wasn't going away. As a matter of fact, these tunnels seemed dustier than those they had crawled through at first, though it was hard to tell after so long. Nirrin's neck was getting a crick from trying to see ahead, where there was nothing to see.

"I've got one," Duff whispered. "A grille. I'm opening it now."

No light at all. Well, it could be any sleeping

chamber, any of the smaller corridors. Oil was precious and only the main corridors and detentioin areas were kept lit at sleep time, for emergencies.

There was a muffled rasp as the grille came free.

"Be careful," Nirrin breathed. She was beginning to regret this whole attempt to help Gen. He wouldn't appreciate it, anyway. Gen never showed gratitude to Nirrin, even though she had often —

"Shh!" A soft thud. Duff landed on the floor beneath.

So far, so good. No outcries. No wardens running their way.

"Where are we?" Nirrin whispered.

"I can't tell yet. But speak a little louder and you're bound to wake someone up. Then we'll know!"

"All right. I'll be quiet."

Nirrin wiggled through the opening and dropped to Duff's side. Every sleep time of her life Nirrin had been in the dark. She was not afraid of it, but she knew they dared not alert anyone to their presence. So she moved with care. Cautiously she began to feel around in the dark. If this were her own sleeping chamber, there would be a sleeping platform just here —

Nirrin's hands encountered a shape.

"We've got to get out of here," she breathed.

"There's someone — "

Nirrin held her breath. Beside her, she heard Duff freeze and control his own breathing. There was no other sound. No sleeper's snore . . . and there was something wrong with the texture she had felt. With a sick feeling, she put out her hand again. The blanket under it crumbled. A sharp long shape chilled her hand. Dust rose into her nose. Her fingers travelled up the object, forming a mental picture. A black suspicion entered her mind. Curved objects, now, rows of slender shapes, a ball with some shaggy covering.

"Duff . . . " Nirrin strangled her cry.

"What is it? Why is it so quiet?"

"The person on this platform isn't sleeping. He's dead!"

Duff gasped. He put out his hand. "Bones!" he said. "This is no recent death. Come on."

Nirrin and Duff crept from the room on rubbery legs. They blundered down a dark hall, tripping over unseen things on their way. A distant ray of light drew them. They turned toward it and found a lighted corridor.

A broken panel overhead cast a feeble glow on a litter of nameless objects and broken glass disks.

"It's the other place. We've come through, but into a different hall," Duff said.

Nirrin gulped air, steadied herself. "It's true, then. There is a place outside Senedu. I don't like it, though."

"Neither do I. I wonder who — "

"Whoever it was, they won't be reporting us to the wardens." Nirrin realized she was speaking as much for her own benefit as for Duff's. Talking always made her feel better. "Which way now?"

Duff looked at Nirrin. "Are you okay?"

She nodded. "Let's try this direction."

Most of the things on the floor had no purpose that Nirrin could recognize. She didn't want to look too closely. They stepped over and around them and hurried on. This was all taking too long. Nirrin knew it. But what could she do except go on? They didn't know the way back any more.

"Listen!" Duff said.

"That's a peculiar sound."

"Hissing! The voice of the Dragn!" Duff said darkly. "If we follow that we should find Gen."

"Good!"

All the corridors they travelled were filmed with dust, sometimes almost choked with heaps of strange metal objects, smashed beyond recognition. The magic light panels were seldom intact. The glass disks overhead were dark.

The hissing grew louder.

They ran into dead-end corridors that were much too small for storage chambers. What were they for?

Duff and Nirrin doubled back, got lost again, had to turn once more toward a blocked tunnel.

"The voice is coming from behind that wall. We can't get any closer."

Nirrin found an air shaft grille and pried it loose.

"I hate these tunnels!" she muttered. "You go first."

"We're not going to make it, are we?" Duff said quietly. "We'll never get back before lamplight. It must be later than that already."

Nirrin bit her lip. "I'm sorry I got you into this, Duff."

Duff shrugged and smiled faintly. "I was already in it. Besides, I was the one who got lost."

He boosted himself into the air tunnel and held out a hand to Nirrin. If they followed the sound of the Dragn, they would find Gen soon.

Of course, Nirrin thought savagely, Gen was probably back in his cell now, looking innocent. Well, I've come all this way, I might as well see the beast that's caused all of this trouble.

Gen did ask me to stay out of this.

Chapter 11

If Jered had been more popular, he would have been missed sooner. No one cared that he was absent for breakfast. No one bothered to check on him until he failed to show for his duties at first watch. For one thing, everyone was too busy talking about the escape of the two Rule breakers from the detention cells.

At last an irritated journeyman sent a bored apprentice to fetch the missing farm trainee.

"Tell him he goes on report for this! And hurry, or you'll have his duties to do on top of your own!"

Cal hitched up his belt, the green belt of the farming caverns, and started off down the corridors at a trot. It was just like the new boy to make trouble, though he had never gone this far before. Everyone could see that he had a bad attitude. Bad attitudes brought bad seasons. It was a saying in the green caverns. Light from the lenses, water from the great lake in the Hall of Waters, weeds, fertile mucks and moulds — all were carefully controlled, but still the crop sizes varied. The will of the workers made a difference. There was no other possible explanation.

He passed the kitchen sector and descended the stairs to Level Three — the sleeping chambers. The clatter of dishwashing followed him for more than a few minims. Jered's assigned chamber was 172. It took no more than a glance to see that the cubicle was empty. Curious, Cal stepped over to the sleeping platform. The blankets were not even disturbed. Jered had not slept here! The new apprentice was in big trouble. If he was mixed up with those missing boys —

A flash of white attracted Cal's eyes as he turned to leave. The corner of a letter protruded from the pillow. After a moment's hesitation, Cal took it out. It was addressed to Councillor Arn and sealed. Burning with curiosity, Cal ran toward the Council chamber. He knew better than to open a message intended for a Councillor. Cal had no intention of landing in the detention cells himself!

Chapter 12

Councillor Arn stood. His face was pale.

"I regret to inform the Council that my daughter Nirrin has disappeared."

There were shocked murmurs. The eyes of the Dream Speaker met the eyes of the Guardian across the wide table.

"A search must be made for her of course," the Guardian said.

"A search has been made. Neither she nor the escaped boys have been found anywhere in Senedu."

"The city is large. There are many unused storerooms —"

Arn frowned. "I myself conducted a search before my late arrival at this meeting. The young people are not in Senedu. I give you my word."

"But that's preposterous! They must be in

Senedu. There is no other place!" a Councillor cried.

"There is Senedu, and there is the unformed stone," another said. "That is all. Any child knows this!"

Arn held the eyes of the Guardian, refusing to sit down. "There are the air shafts."

The Guardian nodded. His eyes betrayed no emotion. "Just so. If Nirrin is missing, then she has done the forbidden thing in spite of our warnings. She has gone into the air shafts. These tunnels are unstable. A rock slide must have killed her. I regret that this has happened."

Still Arn would not be seated. "Then let us open up the tunnels and search for her body. The passages can be widened. The miners have the skill to do it, to brace the tunnels as they go. If openings are made above each level and at the junctions — "

The Guardian's voice was like a hammer. "No!"

Arn's face reddened. "This does not affect my daughter alone. It also concerns your son, Guardian."

There were scattered mutters. The Dream Speaker shook her head slightly. The Guardian spoke again.

"Councillor Arn, we have heard your words. We grieve for your loss. I have given you my decision. The matter is closed." Every eye in the

Council chamber turned to see how Arn would respond. He remained standing.

"I claim Council privilege — the right to speak in emergencies!" There was a square set to Arn's shoulders that suddenly made him look much like his older brother.

"No emergency has been declared!" the Guardian cried over the rumble of surprise in the room.

"I declare one now!"

The Guardian stifled a word. By custom he could not stop Arn from speaking, but by virtue of their relationship, he still tried.

"You will destroy the Balance!" he said sternly.

"If the Balance does not allow the truth, then perhaps it would be better destroyed."

At this there were outraged gasps. No such blasphemy had been spoken in the Council chamber in living memory.

The Dream Speaker stood, her ancient eyes blazing. "The Guardian is the keeper of Truth. We need no other."

Several Council members nodded and looked to see how the Guardian would respond. He made a gesture of sympathy, of reason in the face of panic.

"Enlarge the air shafts and they will become more unstable," he declared. "From time to time Senedu has endured earth tremors. It has stood firm. I will not allow the structure to be undermined. The Good of Senedu outweighs my love for my son. The matter is closed!"

"Then send the smaller members of our community to find out what has happened. What harm can there be in that?"

"What harm? To risk more lives? Councillor, sit down!"

Arn's jaw worked. "Gen and Nirrin are no fools! They may be injured, trapped, unable to call for help. But I cannot believe they are dead. Guardian, why won't you allow a search? Is there something in the air shafts that we must not see? Is that it?"

"Ridiculous!"

"Crazed!"

"Councillor, be silent!" The Guardian's voice would have cowed another. Arn simply took a paper from his tunic pocket and unfolded it.

"I wished to avoid reading this in Council. Now I feel that I must," he said. "Jered left this note for me. Some of you will remember that Jered was a mining apprentice and has recently been transferred to the green caverns. He did not report for his duties at first watch today. A search was made. He too is missing."

The Guardian's granite face reflected uncertainty. Arn read the note aloud.

"You know, Councillor Arn, that I am no spreader of wild tales. I was trained as a miner until transfer to the farming caverns. I have my feet on the stone.

"You also know I reported Gen and Duff for doing the forbidden thing — climbing in the air shafts.

"Perhaps I did wrong.

"Gen found corridors that are not part of Senedu. He saw a Dragn. At least, that is what he says.

"Gen believes Senedu is in great danger. He asked me to tell you. I am going now to see if his story is true. If you read this letter, then you know that something has prevented me from coming back. Warn the Guardian.

"I am Jered. I am no dreamer of dreams. I tell the truth."

The Councillors broke into speech all at once. Outrage, consternation, surmise, disbelief — so many feelings erupted at once that none of them could be understood.

Across the chaos, Arn saw a look of wild surmise flash across the Guardian's face. Then it was gone.

The Dream Speaker drew herself to her feet. "These are the fantasies of children! There are no Dragns! Jered was deceived, but we are too wise to listen to these lies."

"Then let us find Gen and the others, search the tunnels, find the thing that so frightened them," said Arn.

The Guardian stood. From long custom, all voices were stilled. He raised the Wand of Authority. The metal rod glittered coldly. The Guardian's face had become a mask of iron.

"Gen, Guardian-to-be, Duff, son of Dafid, and Nirrin, daughter of Arn, are dead. They are not of the People. Jered, son of Jerrit, also is not of the People."

The Councillors looked up, appalled. The Guardian had begun the ritual of un-naming, of casting out. If he declared the children outcasts, no one could search for them, no one could speak to them, should they return, and no one could even say their names aloud without risking the same fate.

"They are not of the People."

The Guardian was cutting them off from all aid or human contact. An outcast could enter a room, but none of the People would ever acknowledge his presence. No place would ever be set for him at the tables. Outcasts seldom lived more than a season. "No!" Arn hissed. "Gen's your own son! And Nirrin is my daughter!"

The Guardian ignored him. The words of the ritual passed his stony lips. "The People cast them out." He lowered the Wand.

In a flat voice the Guardian brought the Council meeting to an end. The matter of the missing young people had been made taboo. Arn made his way to the door. Powerful emotions played across his face. A few Councillors covertly touched his arm as he passed. They dared not do more.

Arn had taken the biggest gamble of his life. And he had lost. The Guardian had spoken of casting out his own son, but Arn had not really thought him capable of it. Without that extreme measure, the debate would have continued. A little more time and Arn might have persuaded the Council to his point of view. The air tunnels would have been opened, explored. Nirrin and Gen might have been found and saved. All the young people might have been saved. For Arn was sure they were in danger — alive, but in grave danger. If there really was a Dragn, all of Senedu was in danger. What did the Guardian intend to do about it?

Hamar, representative of the green caverns, and Sarin, a masterweaver, had always been Arn's friends. He had sensed some support in them, before the debate was cut off. Sarin was a strong woman with her own sons. She would have voted for the search. And Quig, master-builder, had lost a boy to the wasting disease. He had more than a little sympathy for Gen.

Why? Why had the Guardian done it? Was he really ready to let his own son suffer and perish in some unknown place rather than let the miners explore the air shafts? It made no sense! If there really was a Dragn in the air tunnels, then surely the Guardian would wish to find it — would have to find it for the sake of Senedu. It almost seemed that he was afraid to look. What was it the Guardian so desperately sought to hide?

The Guardian was Arn's brother, but Arn could not understand him. Certainly, there had been many secret meetings between their father and the Guardian. There were things never told to the younger brother. Arn had always assumed these were matters of ritual, custom.

Perhaps there had been something more.

The years had weighed heavily on the Guardian. When Arn looked across the Council table now, he saw a stranger with closed eyes and a stern, unmovable face.

What burden could be so heavy? What secret so terrible? Was there really a Dragn?

Arn returned to his own chamber. The lives of his daughter and the other young people were in Arn's hands. No one else would help them. But what could he do now? Without the Guardian's support, no new diggings could be made. Arn was much too big to follow the children into the air shafts. He could not ask anyone else to do it, either.

He thought of Nirrin's mother, who had died in childbirth. How he wished she were here now to help him.

Had he been defeated?

Chapter 13

"This is it," Duff declared. "This is the right way now."

"Finally," Nirrin sighed. "How can you be sure?"

"The shape of the tunnels. The feel of the rock outcroppings. I remember them. If I can trust myself!"

Nirrin sucked on a scraped knuckle. It was completely dark in this part of the tunnels. They were far away from Senedu now. And the dead corridors had been left behind, thank goodness! "I hate tunnels," Nirrin muttered. "Okay, let's go."

She crawled deftly after Duff. Something scurried away from her — probably a long-leg. Yuck!

"How far now?"

"Not far. Listen. Do you hear that sound? It is the Dragn's voice!"

Nirrin frowned. She did hear something new. A sort of hissing, as if a large beast slept in the tunnels ahead. Or spoke. But how could anyone translate such a word? Was it really a Dragn? Straining to understand the sound, Nirrin heard something else.

"Shh! There's someone else in the tunnel with us! I hear voices."

Should they go on or turn back? The voices were muted. Nirrin couldn't be sure of what they said. But there was something familiar about the sound of one . . .

"Gen?" Nirrin called.

"Hello? Who's there?" came the muffled reply.

Duff and Nirrin raced ahead.

"Gen, why are you still here?" Nirrin cried. "Do you know how angry the Guardian is?"

"Who are — Nirrin?" Gen never thought he would be glad to hear Nirrin's voice, but this time he was.

"Gen, are you hurt?" Duff called.

"No, but we need help."

"Go on," Nirrin urged. "They're farther ahead."

"I can't go on," Duff said quietly. "The tunnel is blocked!"

"What?"

It took little time to explain what had happened.

"Can you dig us out?"

"I think so."

"You'll have to be careful. The tunnel is unstable. Have you anything to use as a brace?" said Gen.

"The stones here can be wedged, I think."

"We're being rescued by children?" Jered sounded incredulous.

"We could go back for help," put in Duff.

There was a long pause. Nirrin broke the silence at last. "Duff and I got lost coming here and used up a lot of minims. It must be the second watch already. I'm afraid we'll just be arrested if we go back now."

"We need miners, not children!" Jered said.

"Miners can't fit in these tunnels, even if they were given permission to come. And I don't think the Guardian would give permission," Nirrin said.

Gen had noticed a stale taste to the air in the closed part of the tunnel. How much longer could they safely wait?

"I think they should give it a try, Jered."

Reluctantly, he agreed.

Working by feel in the darkness, Duff and Nirrin gently shifted stones. It was painstaking, terrifying work. One false move and the tunnel could cave in on top of them all. The larger stones were almost too heavy to move at all. They worked from the top down, creating a supportive arch with the debris, against one side of the tunnel.

"I hate closed spaces," Nirrin muttered as she squeezed next to Duff to wedge a rock into position. She reached for another loose stone.

"This isn't a rock. This is a shoe."

They had broken through.

Duff guided Jered through the gap. It seemed at first that he would not fit. He had to turn sideways, and he left skin and torn clothing on more than one stone.

"You call that a brace?" he gasped.

"Some people would speak respectfully to persons who had just rescued them!" Nirrin said.

"Let's get clear of this area," Gen interrupted. "We don't want to trigger another rockfall. Then maybe you can tell me what you're doing here."

They edged backward in the tunnels.

"You might sound a little more grateful," Nirrin grumbled.

"I am grateful!" Gen took a deep breath. "Only — "

"We came to warn you about — " Nirrin broke off, then sighed. "I guess I'd better tell you the worst. Your father threatened to outcast you if you pulled any more stunts like this. I thought if you could get back in time. . . "

"The Guardian outcast his own son!" Jered scoffed. "You must be joking!"

There was an uncomfortable silence. Gen was glad no one could see his face in the dark.

"Thank you," he said roughly. "For rescuing us and for the . . . warning. It's a little late to cover up this 'stunt,' though. It must be well past lamp-light." His voice strengthened. "But it isn't too late to warn the Council about the Dragn."

"I still don't believe — " Jered began.

"I can make you believe," said Gen. "If you dare follow me."

"Dare?" Jered snapped.

"Nirrin, you'd better stay here. There's no need for you — "

"Are you crazed? Me stay here while you do all the exploring?"

"All right," Gen said heavily. "We'll all stay together then."

They crept back in the tunnel until they found the side passage Gen remembered.

"This way," he called.

"That hissing," Nirrin said. "It's getting louder."

"The Dragn," Gen explained. "We're close now."

They turned toward a distant light and climbed.

"I'm not really sure I want to see this," Nirrin mumbled.

Gen stopped. "Then you can stay — "

"Go on, go on. I told you I'm coming. You don't listen very well."

"Don't worry. There won't be anything to see," Jered snapped.

"Through here."

Gen had reached a grille. White light flooded the tunnel as he levered it open.

He dropped into a corridor brightly lit by the mysterious panels that had no flame. And here the circles of glass also pulsed with a yellow light. Hissing vibrated through the air.

"This is like the dead corridors," said Nirrin. She shuddered.

Gen wanted to ask her what she meant, but the Dragn's voice had become a powerful summons. It drowned the senses. At the end of the corridor Gen thought he saw a glint of pale skin. The Dragn's lair! They must go quickly, see the Dragn, and then escape to warn the People. Too much time had already passed. Gen steadied himself. The adults would have to believe if four of them reported the same thing!

"The truth of my tale is through that door. Come with me now," Gen said grimly. If they were quiet, the Dragn might not see them.

And he started down the corridor.

Nirrin exchanged a glance with Duff.

"Why take the risk?" Duff said. "You believe us, don't you?" Jered's tunic was streaked with sweat and dirt. He reached out a hand to touch the unnaturally smooth walls. His fingers left a smear of blood. His eyes narrowed.

"This could still be a trick," Jered said. "Show me."

In the midst of the corridor a door suddenly slid shut. "What?" Gen exclaimed.

He backed away from the door, alert for danger.

"How did you do that, Guardian-to-be?" Jered snapped. He stepped to the door and tried to force it open. There were no handles, gaps or imperfections to grip. As solid as stone it stood, separating them from the Dragn. But it was not stone. And it would not move. Magic! Jered pounded the door with a bloodied fist. He turned to where Gen stood.

"Lies, all the time! You brought me here only to betray me."

Gen shook his head. "No, Jered."

"Well you've had your revenge, and welcome to it!" Jered cried. "Now can we get out of here?"

"You don't really believe that Gen closed that door without touching it!" Nirrin cried. "Jered, none of us knows Elder magic."

She stared at the door with misgiving.

"But if you didn't trigger the magic door, who did?" Jered snapped.

"I don't know," Gen said. He was badly shaken, but he didn't want to give Jered the satisfaction of seeing it.

Someone else was in the tunnels with them! Someone silent, hidden. Someone who knew magic and could control the doors. The Dragn had spoken to Gen once, but it was a monster.

Could a beast reason and seal doors? Surely not! But if not the Dragn, then who?

Every instinct in Gen told him there was a new mystery here.

"This doesn't make sense!" Jered growled. He began to recite the words of the Truth Time and other ceremonies that preserved the history of Senedu. He spoke of the Elders and the Beginning Time. He paced the alien corridor. "This place doesn't fit in!"

"I know," Gen said.

"We shouldn't have come back," Duff said.

"This place is not of the People. That's certain," Nirrin decided. "It shouldn't even exist. According to our teachers there is unformed stone beyond Senedu — nothing! Either our teachers are wrong — the Guardian, the Council, everyone is wrong, or . . ." Nirrin met Gen's eyes.

"Or they are lying." Gen finished the thought.

"I can't believe — ! They wouldn't dare — !" Jered shook his head. Something dawned in his eyes. "That's it, isn't it? That's why you are in the lockup! Because you have discovered a different truth!"

Gen nodded.

"They're never going to let you out. They can't," Jered said slowly. "Not you, not Duff, not me, not any of us." The anger drained from Jered's face, leaving it pale. "You knew it was this bad, didn't you? Why did you let me come?" But before Gen could answer, Jered spoke again. "I invited myself, didn't I?" He gave a strained smile. "They'll lock us up and throw away the keys."

"If we ever get back through those tunnels," Duff said.

Jered stared at Gen. "The Council would take it as a favour if we stayed lost permanently. But I wouldn't! Even a mucker is better off than a dead man."

"We have to get back! And we have to escape the detention cells," Gen said, determination in his dark eyes. "Otherwise, who will warn the People about the Dragn?"

"Oh, yes, the monster. I had nearly forgotten." Jered grimaced.

"Someone shut us in here," Gen declared. "And someone is going to let us out. Hello!" he shouted. "Why have you done this?"

To Gen's astonishment, a cold voice answered.

"I cannot allow you to come any closer. You have not identified yourselves."

Chapter 14

Arn sat in his chamber creating and then abandoning new plans. With the Guardian against him, how could he do anything to help his daughter and his nephew and the others? Four young people — perhaps trapped and injured somewhere in the air shafts — and the Guardian refused to help. And one of them his own son! It made no sense!

At the third watch, someone knocked on Arn's door.

"Enter!"

The woman who opened the door was known to Arn — Illys, Jered's mother and a skilled toolmaker. Behind her stood Hamar, the big-boned veteran farmer, Duff's father, Dafid, Sarin, masterweaver and Quig, masterbuilder. Illys faced Arn stiffly. "I intend to speak of my son. If you choose not to listen, say so now."

Arn rose to his feet.

"I will listen."

Chapter 15

The strange voice shocked all of the children. They stood frozen for a minim. Then they looked for the one who had spoken. In the whole alien corridor, no one else could be seen.

"Where are you?" Gen called.

"They sent out a search party after all," Duff decided. "Your father does — "

"This is no search party!" Gen interrupted gruffly.

"Gen," Nirrin said, "there is no one else here!"

"He's hiding," Jered said.

"There's no place to hide!"

It was true. There was no rubble here, no overturned boxes or furniture behind which a man could crouch.

The voice was cold. But whoever the speaker was, he didn't seem angry. That was strange. The wardens would be furious. Gen was sure this was no warden.

It was impossible to tell the age of the voice,

and it seemed to come from all directions at once. There was a prickling at the base of Gen's spine.

"I assure you, I am here," the voice continued.

"Who are you?" Gen cried.

"I am the Wizard."

"What!" Jered growled. "The Wizards are all dead! The Elders threw them down, destroyed them. Even a baby knows that!"

"I am still alive," the cool voice replied.

"Gen!" Duff said. "The Wizards were evil! You know that!"

"So the teachers say," Nirrin murmured. "But they say many things, don't they?"

"Who are you?" the Wizard asked.

"Don't listen to him, Gen!" Duff urged. "We must leave here now! We cannot deal with these sacred matters."

"This fellow is a sneak and a liar," Jered decided. "Only that kind is afraid to talk face to face. And he's no Wizard!"

"Why are you hiding?" Gen called.

There seemed to be amusement in the voice. "I am not hiding."

"Then show yourself! If you want us to trust you, let us see you."

"You refuse to tell me your names until you see me?"

"Yes."

"Very well."

The lights went out. For the blink of an eye, the children were plunged into darkness, lit only by the pulsing disks on the ceiling. Gen held his breath. Then the corridor was flooded with light again. An old man stood at its end, before the door. He was tall — taller than any of the People of Senedu. His hair and beard were grizzled. Age covered him like his close-fitting grey garment. But his eyes sparkled with interest.

Gen had never seen anyone so old. Relief coursed through him. At least the Wizard was a man! For a moment he had wondered . . . but how could a man exist outside of Senedu for season upon season as this man had done?

"Now you see me." The ancient mouth smiled. "Who are you?"

"Gen, son of the Guardian, Jered, son of Jerrit, Duff, son of Dafid, and Nirrin, daughter of Councillor Arn."

The Wizard looked thoughtful. "Not all these names are on my list, but that is to be expected. You will have to give me the proof yourselves."

"What proof can we offer? We brought nothing with us."

"What does he want?" Nirrin asked.

"You misunderstand." The Wizard stepped to a featureless wall and waved a hand. "Perhaps this will help."

On the wall, rows of letters and numbers appeared. The Wizard might have been teaching a spelling lesson or a set of sums. The Wizard stepped back, keeping his distance from the children.

"How did he do that?" Jered said.

"More magic," added Duff. "Don't trust him, Gen. Don't go any closer. Think! What do we know about magic? How can we fight it?"

Gen approached the wall.

"The Guardian game," Nirrin said. "Gen, it's like your game board!"

"How do you know that?" Gen asked.

Nirrin shook her head. "That doesn't matter. I always wondered what it meant. Go on, play it!"

"Duff's right. The old man isn't to be trusted. Stay back," Jered rasped.

Gen looked at the Wizard. "Wizards and Dragns . . . " he began. All his life he had been taught to hate and fear them. Fear — yes. Gen feared the Wizard because he was unknown. But this old man did not look evil. Indeed, his eyes showed a gentle spirit, and intelligence. He had done no evil. What should Gen do? Time was passing — precious minims that could never be recovered. Gen spoke again. "We want to warn our people about the Dragn. Let me show my friends."

"Yes, of course you must warn them. But I cannot let you into the Dragn's chamber unless you can prove yourselves."

Gen looked into the lively eyes of the old man

and made his choice. He stepped up to the game board pattern on the wall. "No!" Duff blurted out. "It's a trick. The Wizard will harm you. How can anyone who serves a Dragn be trusted?"

Swiftly, Gen touched letters and numbers in a dizzying pattern. He half expected to be struck down. But that didn't happen. Instead, the Wizard smiled.

"Welcome. I have been waiting for you. I need your help. Please follow these stairs."

A door slid back where the wall had seemed to be solid stone. A circular staircase was revealed descending into the depths. The hissing of the Dragn grew into an avalanche of sound. The Wizard stepped onto the staircase and vanished.

Gen took a deep breath. "We're nearly there. Come on."

"Gen, wait! Look at the floor."

Where the children had stepped, footprints disturbed the dust of many seasons. But where the Wizard had stood, there was no mark at all.

Chapter 16

Arn quickly closed the door of his sleeping cubicle. He turned to Jered's mother, Illys, and the Councillors.

"You realize what you risk by coming here?"

Hamar the farmer gave a crooked grin. "We come to visit a grieving friend. That is all. Should we be questioned by the wardens, we will testify to that."

So, the whole group was sworn to secrecy. Some of the worry fell from Arn's shoulders. Still, if any outsider overheard them, all of them could be outcast.

"Did any wardens see you come?"

"No. The halls were empty of guards."

Arn frowned. "That is strange. I would have thought — " But why should Arn complain? For whatever reason the Guardian had withdrawn the guards from the halls, it gave Arn some privacy to talk of forbidden things.

Illys gripped Arn by the shoulder. "We cannot let our children die without a fight!"

There were muttered agreements. Quig caught Arn's eye. "But there is more to this than the loss of your children. The questions you brought up in Council . . . "

"Do you think you are the only one to ask yourself what is beyond Senedu?" asked Hamar.

"A dangerous question!"

A crafty look came over Hamar's square face. "What question?"

"The Guardian holds the reins of power over-tight lately," Quig rumbled.

"He has knowledge he refuses to share with us. Why?"

Sarin, a tall woman with clear grey eyes, spoke. "Whatever he hides, it is important. To keep it hidden, he is willing to sacrifice his son."

"And your daughter," Illys said to Arn. "My son Jered is stubborn and angry. But he is no fool. If he went with Gen, Duff and Nirrin, there was a good reason."

"Let us consider the consequences," Arn said slowly. "If we move against the Guardian's will, we will disrupt the Balance." The others nodded.

"That is the main reason I have kept quiet all these years," said Quig. "Without strong discipline, Senedu cannot survive. The Guardian is the heart of this discipline."

"If we win, chaos results," Hamar rumbled unhappily.

"If we lose, we all become outcasts. So many outcasts have never been seen at once in Senedu. I don't know what the Guardian would do."

"He could not let us live. We hold too much respect in our caverns," Quig said grimly.

Arn nodded. "Once, ages ago, a small group was exiled — turned out of Senedu to die. They were never heard of again."

"Turned out where? You see the problem. How can anyone be exiled if there is nowhere else to go?"

"Empty, poisoned caverns? The remains of the destroyed Sky cavern?"

"Away from Senedu and its farms, its hall of waters . . . " Quig grunted. "I am not in a hurry to die, or to be exiled! Neither do I wish to stand idle while four young people perish."

"They may already be dead," Dafid said softly. It was the first time the man had spoken. His face was filled with grief. "I do not wish others to die for the sake of my son, no matter how much I mourn his loss."

Arn shook his head sharply. "No! I do not believe they are dead! Not yet. They know the ways of the caverns. They are in trouble, yes. This I believe."

"So what can we do to help them? We cannot crawl around in the air shafts like children. The shafts are too small," said Sarin.

Arn took a deep breath. "Somewhere in Senedu there is a door, carefully hidden. A door to other places. The exiles must have been forced to pass through it. We must find that door!"

So the agreement was made. One by one, the parents and the Councillors left Arn's chamber and scattered throughout Senedu. They examined walls, ceilings, floors. They travelled the corridors of Senedu from end to end.

But they found no door.

Arn returned to his chamber heavy with fatigue. Dimly he wondered why there was no warden on duty outside his door. But he was too tired to give the matter much thought.

How, how could he help Nirrin and Gen?

Chapter 17

The opening to the Dragn's lair gaped like the jaws of a beast. Inside, a stairway twisted downward, shrouded in shadows. Gen looked at Nirrin. No one moved for a minim.

"That was no ordinary man," Jered growled. "The Wizard left no footprints in the dust. I told you he couldn't be trusted!"

Gen shook his head stubbornly. "We don't understand him. That doesn't mean he cannot be trusted."

Duff frowned at the winding staircase that had been revealed. "You're not going down there! You mustn't!"

"And you, Nirrin. What do you think?"

"Suddenly you want to know what I think?" Nirrin smiled feebly.

Gen shrugged. "You notice things."

"The Wizard is not what he seems. He's

hiding something. How did he enter the corridor? We didn't hear the door open. If he were a man of Senedu, he would have disturbed the dust. He knows great magic. I agree with Jered."

Gen was disturbed by this, too. Was he wrong about the Wizard? If so, he was leading his friends from danger into death. And for the Good of Senedu! Was he any different from his father?

"We have to go on. The Wizard controls the doors. We cannot find the Dragn again without his help. I am willing to try the stairs," Gen said. "I need you to be witnesses, but I won't force you to come."

Gen turned to Jered. "What do you say?"

"No orders? No commands?"

"None."

Jered looked uncomfortable. "Let's go, then."

Nirrin tried to grin. "Well, I am curious . . ."

Duff shook his head. "Someone had better come to keep you fools out of trouble."

They entered the gaping threshold and began to descend. The stairs twisted downward. There was no sign of the Wizard. Walking or floating, he must have gone on ahead.

The voice of the Dragn throbbed in the air.

There was a coiled knot of tension inside Gen. How could the People fight anything as big and powerful as the Dragn? Even if they believed Gen and the others, what could they do? Why was the Wizard allowing them to approach the beast's lair? What help did he need? There were too many unanswered questions. Perhaps the Wizard could not be trusted. In that case, Gen was leading them all to death. By what right? Because he was Guardian-to-be? If that was the reason, Gen wanted nothing to do with it!

How terrible to have to make decisions that might save or kill other people. Gen had a sudden, sickening insight into the burden his father carried every day. He was appalled.

But something like the Dragn could not be ignored. It was too close to Senedu. It was too deadly. Someone had to sound the alarm. Others, stronger perhaps, would have to seek it out, learn its weaknesses — if it had any. Fight it! Gen was doing what he must. He only hoped he was right.

Gen's legs were tiring. With a soft shushing sound, a door in the wall slid open. Beyond was a flash of pale skin and a shuddering in the air — the Dragn. In spite of himself, Gen hesitated.

"Do not be afraid," the cold voice of the Wizard said. "Enter. See the Dragn. It will not harm you."

So the Wizard had descended the stairs ahead of them. There he stood, his old face creased in a smile. "Stay here," Gen told the others. "If it doesn't harm me, you can follow."

That was the least he could do. And it took all of his courage. He stepped into the monster's lair. It neither moved nor changed its menacing song. High overhead the Dragn's bulk loomed — a giant beyond all imagining, a tower of fear. The smoke of its fiery breath plumed far above.

Behind him, Gen heard the others gasp.

"It's true!" Nirrin said.

"I never would have believed — " Jered rasped. "You've got me now, Guardian-to-be. I'm convinced. Let's get out of here before the beast decides to have us for breakfast."

"No!" the Wizard cried. "Not until you have done what I ask!"

Gen guessed what would happen next. He was beginning to know this Wizard. The door to the stairs slid shut. There was no way out. They were in the power of the Wizard and the Dragn.

"Now I will tell you a story," the Wizard said.

The old man smiled. His smile was pleasant. His eyes seemed kind. But he had trapped them in the Dragn's lair. And now he stood between them and their escape.

Chapter 18

Gen stood perfectly still. There was no way out. Beside him, stiff with fear, Nirrin, Duff and Jered caught their breath. The cold voice of the Wizard washed over them. They could not choose but listen.

"This is my story.

"A long time ago, men did not live in caverns. They lived in the open, under the sky."

Gen wondered what the open was, and what the Wizard meant. Surely Sky was the name of the huge cavern the Elders called home?

"Men quarrelled. They made weapons so terrible that they came to fear war."

Now Gen was completely confused. And angry — too angry to keep quiet.

"What is war?"

The Wizard's voice fell silent for a moment.

"The men you call the Elders would be happy

to know you have forgotten the meaning of that word. It means that many people fought each other, killed each other."

People killing People! What was the matter with their Guardians? Gen thought.

"Why?"

The Wizard looked sad as he answered.

"I do not know. Some wanted things other men owned. In some places, there were more people than there was food to feed them. In other places, men ate so much that they grew fat. But this is only part of the answer.

"Let me go on with my story.

"This place, all of Senedu, was built so that some men could survive a war and send weapons to destroy the enemy.

"Do you know the meaning of the word 'Senedu'?" the Wizard asked.

"It means home. It has no other meaning," Jered grunted.

"It is a short form for a longer name," the Wizard said. "Sealed Environment Experimental and Defense Unit."

"What?" Nirrin breathed.

A cold emptiness seemed to yawn at Gen's feet. The past, everything he knew and thought he understood, tilted away from him, slid toward an abyss. I can stop this, Gen thought. I can make the Wizard stop his story. I can keep out his words.

But another part of Gen felt a great opening inside — as if barriers in place too long were dissolving away. If there was a truth here, Gen wanted to hear it.

"One hundred and thirty-nine men and women were stationed at Senedu. They began the gardens, the water purifying systems, the recycling of air. They did not expect to stay.

"Then war came. A signal was sent from the command centre. The doors were sealed. The people of Senedu could not leave, even if they wished to.

"They listened to reports from outside. They learned that the air outside had been poisoned by the weapons of the enemy. They were given orders to send their own weapons — their own Dragns, to destroy this enemy.

"I know that your culture has deteriorated to a primitive level. I am putting this as simply as I can."

Some words passed through Gen's mind without conveying any meaning. But a picture began to form itself there — a picture so horrifying that Gen's fear of the Dragn receded before it. "What are weapons?"

"Tools made by men to destroy other men. Three Dragns — three missiles — were launched. Then something happened. Some of the people of Senedu rebelled. They took over control rooms. They refused to fire the last missile. They wanted to stop the war.

"I have listened to your conversation since you came to these corridors. You call these people your Elders. They sealed off this part of Senedu. They adapted to their new life. They tried to forget what had gone before.

"You are the children of their children."

The voice of the Wizard echoed in the Dragn's lair. Nirrin, Duff, Jered and Gen were too stunned to move.

"Lies!" Duff said.

"What better way to forget the past than to rewrite it?" the Wizard asked. "And make any other story a crime to be punished."

"All this time we have learned the wrong truth," Nirrin murmured.

"How long — ?" Gen's voice faltered. "How long ago?"

"There was once a measurement of time called a year. Do you know it?"

Gen shook his head. "No. We measure time in seasons and watches and minims."

"A season is the time it takes for crops to mature?"

"No. In every season two crops mature and the fields lie fallow for a space."

"Then all this happened more than six hundred seasons ago." It was a number too large for comprehension. Gen tried without success to understand its size.

"But they made a mistake," Gen said finally. "The Elders." The blasphemy sounded strange in Gen's ears. The Elders make a mistake?

"Yes," the Wizard said. "They thought the last missile would stand here harmless to the end of time. But poisons leaked through from the surface and activated it.

"This Dragn — the last Digital Remote A-series Guided Neutralizer — is, as you would say, alive. And it is extremely dangerous. If it is not deactivated, the next earth tremor will cause it to explode — to catch fire. And all of Senedu will be destroyed.

"That is why I need your help. You must climb up the missile and reprogram it by hand. By this I mean alter the commands which the Dragn obeys. The circuits have been damaged. I cannot do it."

"What does he mean?" Duff asked. "Why is he telling us these lies?"

So Duff too feels the world he has known slipping away forever, Gen thought. A sense of urgency made Gen crush his own fear, set it aside to be dealt with some other time. The doubts Gen had experienced, the anger he had felt at Truth Time, the unexplained words and concepts — all of it seemed to click suddenly into place. This story, as fantastic as it seemed, somehow made sense. Gen felt its truth within him.

He had heard the worst the Wizard could tell, and he believed.

Gen put his own certainty into words.

"The Wizard is not lying."

And this new truth was terrible. Senedu was in the gravest danger.

"The Dragn is not a beast, as you think," the Wizard said. "If it were a beast, it would have turned and attacked you by now. The Dragn is a thing made by men. And only men can unmake it. Will you help me? Will you climb it?"

"Climb it?" Nirrin exclaimed. "Climb that?"

"I say we get away from this lunatic before he can do anything else to us," Jered growled.

"Haven't you been listening?" Gen said. "If we leave, who will save Senedu from the Dragn?"

"Well, three half-grown weeds and one apprentice can't fight this thing!" Jered snapped. "This Wizard isn't one of the People." He raised his voice. "Climb it yourself, old man! If you are telling the truth, then show us your magic."

The Wizard vanished. The cool voice spoke. "Very well. I took this form to put you at ease." A door beyond the Dragn opened. "Come and see me as I am."

"Don't go, Gen," Duff said. "This Wizard tricks us with magic. He is evil!"

"What evil has he done to us? It seems to me he is trying to help. Can a man be condemned as evil for that?"

Perhaps the Wizard was crippled — that was why he couldn't climb the missile himself. Perhaps he was deformed and didn't want to frighten them with his appearance. So he made a magic image of himself. What difference did it make why he needed help? He needed it. Senedu needed it. If the Wizard wanted to kill them, why go to all this trouble?

Gen decided he didn't care how the Wizard looked. Gen wanted to save Senedu. That came first. If he had the courage to do it. Gen took a deep breath. He stepped through the vast muttering and the fear in the air toward the Dragn. He reached out a hand to touch it.

Its skin was cold — as cold as death. The vibration of its voice travelled up Gen's hand and threatened to drain away what little courage he had. He bit his lip. He began to walk around the monster. Still it did not move.

"It doesn't matter what a person looks like," Gen said. "I am ready, Wizard. If I climb, can you tell me what to do?"

"Yes."

There — handholds set into the skin of the Dragn, leading up, up into the impossible heights. Gen set his hands to the metal rungs and began to climb.

"He's going up!" Jered's voice was almost drowned out by the Dragn's, but in it Gen could hear overwhelming surprise.

"No living thing has metal parts," Gen said, half to convince himself. "This is a tool, made by men." He raised his voice. "Wizard, I am climbing now."

"The task will require some strength, and great accuracy."

Voices from below drifted up to Gen. They had an unreal quality.

"Where do you think you're going?" Jered asked someone.

"I'm going with Gen. We can't let him go alone. He might need help," said Nirrin.

"And you expect to help him? A girl! Wait. I'll probably have to rescue you, too!"

"Doesn't anyone here have a particle of sense?" grumbled Duff.

Gen heard Jered swearing beneath him. He looked down. Behind him both Nirrin and Jered climbed. Duff began to climb, too. They were all following Gen. Gen felt torn — comforted to know he was not alone, and afraid that the others might get hurt. He wanted to shout, "Go back! Don't risk yourselves any more!" Then he thought, They have made their choice. I have no right to take it away from them. He gave them a strained smile.

The floor below seemed to spin. Gen decided not to look down again.

"Try not to fall on my head, Guardian-to-be!" Jered called. They struggled up the missile.

Gen's hands began to sweat. They slipped on the rungs, almost sending him sliding into oblivion. He paused to wipe them on his tunic. That meant Nirrin had to pause, too.

"Keep going," Jered said. There was tension in his voice. Gen set his feet in the next rungs. His hands reached up. Try not to think about it, he told himself. And don't look down! Soon he had recovered his rhythm.

The floor was distant now. But the voice of the Wizard seemed as close as ever. "You are halfway there."

"Thank you for coming, Jered, Nirrin, Duff."

"Don't flap your lips. Climb!"

"Concentrate on what you're doing."

"I hate this. Compared to this, the tunnels were fun."

The angle of the monster changed. It was easier for Gen to keep his balance now. At last he came to the top of the Dragn. There were no jaws. There were no eyes. Smoke seeped from a small hole in the skin of the missile. The hole was discoloured, ragged. Gen knew it should not be there. Below it, a plate was set into the nose of the missile. A wheel was at its centre. "Turn the wheel to your left," the Wizard instructed. "This may be difficult."

Gen tried. He could not budge it.

"It's rusted in place," Nirrin said.

"Here, let me do it."

Jered squeezed past Nirrin. She climbed lower to give him room. Jered took hold of the wheel and applied all of a miner's strength to it.

With a groan of rusted metal, it turned. Suddenly it came free. Jered lurched to the side, lost his grip. Gen reached out. His hands closed on Jered's shoulder as the apprentice swung away from the rungs.

"Hang on!" Gen gasped.

The older boy's weight pulled Gen off-balance. He began to slip. Every muscle cried out as Gen held onto Jered. Then Duff had Jered's legs. The apprentice grabbed for the rungs. He caught the edge of one handhold. He levered himself to safety. But Gen was already off-balance. As Jered gripped the rungs, Gen slid across the monster's nose. Duff lunged for Gen's foot, and fell short.

"Gen!" Nirrin cried.

Gen's fingers struck the edge of the plate. He managed to halt his slide. He dared not even breathe, so precarious was his hold. He looked back at Jered and Duff.

"Don't let go!" Nirrin said.

"I can get you!" Jered called.

But Gen was too far from the rungs now. Jered stretched as far as possible, but he could not reach Gen.

"I can't —"

"A human chain," Nirrin said. "I've done it in

the Hall of Waters, to save a drowning child. We can do it here."

"A girl won't help anything now!" Jered snapped. He strained to reach Gen and again failed.

"She's right," Duff said. "A human chain . . . "

Duff stepped into position beside Jered and began to edge out across the slippery skin of the Dragn.

"Hold Duff — so!" Nirrin instructed.

Duff locked arms with Jered.

"Link your other arm through the rungs. Yes, that's it. Now!"

Nirrin linked arms with Duff. She became an extension of Duff's body, as Duff was an extension of Jered's. Using her hold on Duff to balance, Nirrin let go of the ladder.

"You're all crazed!" Jered grunted.

But he held the others steady. Nirrin reached for Gen. Three links in a human chain — it was enough, barely. "You'll have to reach out to me. You'll have to let go of the plate and reach out your hand!" Nirrin said.

"Careful!" Jered grunted.

The boy who had betrayed Gen, who had put him in a detention cell, and Gen's pesky girl cousin, and Duff, who was opposed to the whole thing — right now Gen's life depended on them. They had bickered every step of the way. Jered had scoffed at Gen. Nirrin had interfered. Duff had argued against this insanity. Gen looked for an instant into their eyes. Jered's face was beginning to go red from the strain. Gen let go of the plate with one hand and reached out. Nirrin seized his hand in a grip surprisingly strong. "Now, pull us back!" Nirrin gasped.

The three moved as one. A heart-stopping moment, and Gen was back on the rungs.

"Well done, herb-girl," Jered panted, and cuffed Duff on the shoulder.

They were all breathing heavily.

"Thank you," Gen said.

He found that his legs were trembling.

"You are safe now? Remove the plate," the Wizard said.

"I'll do it."

Jered's muscles bunched as he wrenched the plate free. A bewildering array of lights and numbers was revealed beneath it. At once a new sound pierced the air — a rhythmic roar. Gen was so startled that he nearly lost his hold on the rungs. The Dragn might have been a beast in pain, warning off those who tore open its silver skin.

"What is — ?" Gen gasped.

An icy mechanical voice interrupted him. It came from the Dragn!

"Countdown sequence initiated. Oh-two hundred and counting . . ."

"Use your key, quickly," said the Wizard. "I

thought this circuit inoperable. A safety device — triggered when an unauthorized person tampers with the missile. I will explain later, when the danger is past. Please — your key!"

"Key? What key?" Gen asked. He found he could not keep his voice steady.

"But you are the General, aren't you?"

"That is my name," Gen said. "And the name of my father before me."

"Then you must have the key!"

"I don't have any key," Gen said. Dread tightened his throat.

There was a terrible pause. Then the Wizard spoke again. "I regret to say I have made a mistake . . . " The voice faltered. "Without the key, you cannot reprogram the missile."

"One hundred and ninety-nine . . . "

"And you cannot stop the countdown. When the missile reaches zero, it will fire, but without proper directions. It will explode here, trapped underground. The great force will destroy Senedu."

"No!" Gen cried.

"Once, the General of Senedu had a key which gave him direct access to many programs. He was required to keep it with him at all times, and to pass it on to his successor. That is why I thought . . . "

"One hundred and ninety-eight. . . "

Gen shook his head, appalled. Senedu was to

be destroyed now! All their efforts to save the city — and they had only brought the end closer! It could not be possible.

"No! We must save the People!"

"There is only one hope for the people of Senedu, now. You must take them away from here. There is a door. . . . Time is short. But if you can get clear of the blast zone . . . "

"Lose Senedu?" Duff rasped. "Lose everything?"

"In order to escape certain death!" the Wizard said.

"He's mucking stupid!" Jered grunted. "How could we build new caverns in time?"

"One hundred and ninety-seven."

"What door?" Gen asked, tension in his voice.

"A door to the outside. From Level One. I do not mean you should escape underground. The air above us is pure, now. The land has been renewed. Men can live again on the surface of this planet."

"What is this 'surface'?" Gen asked. "How do I know the People will be safe there?"

"One hundred and ninety-six."

"We have no time for explanations. It is a good place — a place of large open spaces and many plants. Men lived there before the wars. There will be dangers, yes. But the land is fertile. It will support crops. You must believe me! Go, now! Warn your people. Escape while you can!"

Gen thought of returning to Senedu — collecting the People together, trying to persuade them, even getting them to listen to a discredited boy who had not come of age! And to believe this incredible truth? His heart sank.

"How much — " He could hardly say the words. "How much time before — ?"

"Less than two hundred of your minims."

Less than half a watch! Why, they could barely get back and assemble a meeting in that time! Permission would have to be granted by the Guardian, the Council, each guildmaster . . . Convincing his father alone would be the work of an entire watch! The Guardian's iron face flashed on Gen's inner eye.

"You will come with us," Gen said. "You will help the People to understand."

Perhaps the wisdom of the Wizard would sway the People. Or he could do some magic . . . it was the only hope!

"No. I cannot come. Do not delay any longer. Go!"

Gen caught his breath. "Then you will die when the Dragn catches fire."

"I will die."

Gen had not even seen the Wizard, but everything in him cried out against losing this wise being who had shown him how to save the People.

"There must be another way!"

Chapter 19

"Wait!" Gen told the Wizard. He balanced precariously on the top of the Dragn.

"One hundred and ninety."

The mechanical voice of the Dragn, with its cold promise of death, blurred Gen's thoughts. In less than half a watch Senedu would be destroyed! Gen closed his eyes and concentrated.

Something the Wizard had said . . .

"You say the key was passed on from General to General?"

"Yes."

"And the Guardian — the General, had to keep it with him all the time?"

"That is so."

Gen's eyes met Nirrin's.

"What did it look like?"

"A rod, more than a handspan long, without features."

Nirrin's eyes widened. "The Wand of Authority! Your father never lets it out of his sight. We always thought it was just a symbol . . . "

"We know where it is! We can go back and get it."

"There is no time for that now. You could not reach the city and return in time," the Wizard said. "Again I tell you — save yourselves!"

"You don't know the People," Gen said grimly. "We could reach them in time, yes. But I fear we would all die before I could make them believe in the present danger. To ask them to leave the only world they know . . . ! They have already called me crazed. Besides, we can't leave you here to die. If we could get the wand in time . . . "

"But how?" Jered growled.

"One hundred and eighty-eight."

Don't let the fear cloud your thoughts, Gen told himself sternly. Put aside fear. Put aside doubt. There is a way! Gen thought furiously.

"Wizard!" he called. "You spoke to us in other corridors. Why can't you speak to someone in Senedu? Will your magic reach so far?"

"No. The generals destroyed a part of the machine I use to speak over distances — created a rockfall. Otherwise I would have warned the people of Senedu long ago."

"Supposing we fixed the machine . . . " Gen said. "Would it take long?"

"One hundred and eighty-seven."

If only the missile would stop bellowing its message of death!

"It would take less time than it takes to tell. But you do not understand machines. There was a line to all parts of Senedu. I spoke through it, and I saw through it. The line was broken when Senedu was sealed off from this control room."

"I did not understand the codes, yet I remembered them. Where was the line broken?"

"In the place you call the dead corridors." The Wizard hesitated. "Perhaps it could be done. The tools exist. A simple bypass circuit . . . "

"Duff knows the way," Nirrin said.

"I can project a map for you, also," the Wizard said.

On the featureless wall of the Dragn's lair, a pattern of tunnels and corridors appeared. A path was outlined in red. Farther along the wall, a bay opened. Many metal tools of wonderful craftsmanship were revealed.

"Can you speak to one chamber in Senedu, if we fix the break?" Gen asked.

"Yes."

Gen's eyes met the eyes of Duff, Nirrin, Jered in turn. He saw their understanding.

"What are we waiting for?" Jered rasped. Then he muttered in Gen's ear, "Bepuss sircut?"

"You must follow my directions exactly," said the Wizard. Gen looked up. "I am ready."

Nirrin poked him in the ribs. "We're ready."

Gen swallowed his reply. "Yes."

"One hundred and eighty-five."

The race against death had begun.

Chapter 20

It was time for sleep in Senedu, but Arn did not sleep. He was too troubled to sleep. No door out of Senedu had been found. He did not know how to help his daughter and her friends.

A voice spoke suddenly from the walls. A cold, unfamiliar voice.

"Councillor Arn."

"Who — ?"

"It does not matter who I am. Nirrin and Gen are safe. But they need your help. All of Senedu needs your help. There is not much time!"

This was not possible! A voice out of the walls! The Dream Speaker would say he was crazed. But it was not hard for Arn to make his choice.

Arn slowly rose from the sleeping platform where he had been resting.

"What must I do?"

The voice told him a tale, then, that seemed to be torn from the fabric of nightmares. Terror clutched at Arn. He leapt to his feet and raced for his brother's chambers.

Arn steadied his ragged breathing. He shone his lamp into the door warden's face. The man roused himself with difficulty. Arn forced his face into an expression of calm and his voice into quiet tones.

"Do not trouble yourself, Han. An early message for the Guardian — I will deliver it to him myself," Arn said.

No one else in Senedu would have been allowed to pass unchallenged. The door warden nodded at the Guardian's brother and stretched his aching legs.

If the Guardian awakened now! If the wardens found Arn before he had made good his escape! Arn dared not make a sound.

Precious minims passed while Arn moved stealthily through the gloom. He found the Wand of Authority in the audience chamber, cast down on the desk. Arn hid it in his sleeve and left.

In the next chamber the Guardian listened to the sound of the doors closing. He nodded. It was no longer necessary to pretend to sleep.

Strange, Arn thought, that there is no guard at the head of the stairs. Perhaps, after all, I am safe from the wardens. If I can make it in time . . .

There were no minims now for wondering

why the wardens were not on guard. Later Arn would try to reason everything out. Now, most of Senedu slept. But in a few minims the lamplighters would arise. The first watch would begin. Cooks would hurry to the kitchens, wardens would change duty. The People would pass into the corridors on their way to their assigned duties. Duties they would never complete, unless . . .

Arn must get to Gen!

Arn took the Guardian's rod of office from his sleeve. He looked at the blank wall which blocked the end of the Long Corridor. Nothing distinguished it from any other part of the corridor, except for the smoothness of the wall. No keyhole, no handle . . . Elder work, he had been told.

Arn passed the rod over the top of the door. Nothing happened. He tried both sides. Nothing! Arn's hand shook. He must get through!

Then, as he turned in despair, the rod passed the exact centre of the upper wall panel. It slid open.

"Thank the Elders!"

The light of the oil lamp fell on what first seemed a heap of rubble on the other side of the wall. Arn froze for an instant.

The exiles, Arn realized with a sick feeling.

The rubble was human bones — many bones. The eye sockets of the skulls stared blankly.

Some sound nagged at the edge of Arn's awareness. He was too shocked to notice.

"Their hands!"

The hands of the skeletons were broken. The arms were shattered.

They had died here years ago, trying to open the door — a door forever closed to them because they had dared to question the Guardian's power, Arn thought. As I am doing. Then he shook himself.

"This will not save Senedu!"

"Save Senedu, is it?" a voice sneered. "Listen to the big Councillor talk!"

"Here, what's that hole?"

Arn whirled to face the speakers. On velvet feet a gang of Vandals had approached him. There was no time for this now! Arn turned and tried to leap through the door. One of the gang pounced on him. The Councilman went down with a sickening thud. The Wand of Authority spun off into darkness.

Chapter 21

"You must let me go," Arn gasped. "The safety of Senedu depends on it!"

"And what do we care about the safety of this mucking city?" one of the gang growled.

Arn looked up into the masked face of the boy who sat on him. Arn tensed his muscles, gave a mightly shove. The boy swore and tightened his grip. He was a brawny lad, heavier than Arn and more than a match for a man on the floor.

"This one's slippery, he is! Filthy Council member!"

"Keep him safe, Tiny." The leader of the gang gestured to another member. "You, get that thing he dropped. And you, lift up the lamp. I want a good look at this!"

The boys peered into the black hole that had opened up in the corridor. The leader whistled.

"Something else you mucking Councillors

have hidden from us! You'll be sorry for this!"

"I won't live long enough to be sorry," Arn cried. "And neither will you unless you let me go. This whole city will be destroyed in only a few minims!"

"Lies! More lies! Your kind make me sick! Where does this passage lead?"

"To a Dragn! I swear, I didn't know it myself until tonight. Every minim you keep me here increases the danger!"

The shadowy figure of one of the boys stepped up to the leader with the Wand in his hand. This boy was small, with a thin, pinched voice.

"Look at what he had!" He peered intently at the Wand. "The Guardian's Wand! What were you doing with this?"

"It — it's a key. I opened the door with it."

"You mean there's a way out of this hellhole and you never told the rest of us?" The loathing in the boy's voice made Arn shudder. It was the sound of insane rage barely held back.

"Yes! And I'll show you if the city survives. I promise."

The boy spat. "What good's a promise in your mouth?"

"The freedoms you want, the new life — you'll never have them unless you let me go now." Arn was shouting. Anyone might hear him, and he didn't care. Time! There was no more time! The small boy stammered, "Maybe, maybe we should let him go . . . "

"Have you forgotten? We're Vandals! It's Us against Them! Forever!"

"Yes, but —"

Arn struggled in the stout boy's grip. A sudden bellow sounded in his ear. A blinding light struck his face.

"Release the man!"

The weight on Arn's chest was gone. He lurched to his feet. An agonizing pain shot up his right leg. Arn gasped and stumbled through the door. He bent and retrieved the Wand from the floor where it had been dropped. Then Arn looked up. He saw an enormous, distorted face, floating in the dim corridor. He saw the Vandals scatter — terrified boys at the end. He saw the bones of the exiles snap like twigs as he waded awkwardly through them. But none of these things slowed him down. He was in a race against death and too many minims had already been lost.

Another pass with the rod and the door closed behind him. Almost at once the corridor divided.

"Which way?" Arn gasped.

"You are injured," the Wizard said.

"That doesn't matter."

"I was forced to reveal myself. This could put you at great risk."

"None of that matters now. Which corridor should I follow?"

"Go to the right. And hurry."

How did this unseen man know where Arn was? Where were the eyes that watched him? The nightmare face had vanished, as Arn had somehow expected.

Arn broke into a painful, limping run. He followed the voice of the Wizard, forcing back the pain and the fear, and the doubt. This voice had lured Arn from the safety of Senedu. What if Arn was wrong? There were other bones in the corridors. Had this mysterious voice in the tunnels killed them?

"Why, why didn't the exiles go to your new world?" Arn panted. "Why did they die here, instead?"

"They found nowhere else to go. All this happened many seasons ago. The world was not yet ready for them."

Arn silenced his questions. There would be time for answers later. Perhaps.

"Which way now?" Arn's breath was coming in stifled gasps.

"Straight ahead. You must move more quickly."

Dust and rubble scattered. Arn stumbled on.

No time, no time to rest, to bind his injured leg. Arn laboured painfully up a set of stairs. Magic lights overhead showed him the way.

Then an obscene clanging penetrated the sound of Arn's own rasping breaths. Something shrieked again and again in the alien corridors ahead. Was it a beast bellowing in rage? A deadly, ravening beast?

"What is it?"

"The Dragn," the Wizard replied. "Do not stop. Turn left now."

An icy voice sounded its warning: "Fifty-one."

Then another voice called faintly.

"Father?"

Arn ran toward the sound of his daughter.

Chapter 22

Nirrin caught her father as he lurched along the corridor. Jered was with her.

"The Wand of Authority," Jered grunted.

A quick, questioning look at his daughter and Arn handed it over. Jered took off at a full run down the corridor. Nirrin tried to ease her father to a sitting position.

"No. I want to see," Arn gasped. "Am I in time?"

Nirrin bit her lip. "I don't know."

Arm around his daughter's shoulders, Arn continued his painful progress. Up ahead, Jered's legs were tiring. He was panting with the effort, but he did not slow down. He sprinted to where Duff waited, his hand outstretched.

"Forty-five," the voice of doom echoed.

"Go!" Jered growled.

Smoothly the Wand changed hands. Duff

took up the race. He sprinted toward the Dragn's lair. Three long corridors and then the twisting staircase. Duff had never run so far in his life. His sides ached with the effort.

"Thirty-seven." Had the countdown speeded up, or was it just that fear made it seem so?

Duff saw Gen ahead.

"There may not be enough time," the Wizard's voice said regretfully. "Perhaps you should — "

But Gen had already seized the Wand. He tore across the floor to the missile and up the ladder. Frantically, Gen climbed.

"Won't give up," he panted.

The ladder seemed endless. It vibrated with the forces building up inside the Dragn.

Does death hurt? Gen wondered. He crushed the fleeting thought. Up, up into the dizzying heights.

"Twenty-nine."

With shaking hands, Gen pulled himself up over the shoulder of the missile. He had reached the cone. He took out the Wand of Authority and tried to steady his hand.

Gen passed the Wand over the panel at the top of the Dragn. "Ready to receive new instructions," it said. "Countdown interrupted."

"It — it's stopped!" Gen stammered with relief.

"If you do not complete the reprogramming

in two minims, the countdown will begin again," the Wizard said. "You must not stop. It is essential that you keep going."

"All right."

Gen glanced down. Jered had reached the base of the missile. Nirrin and Duff were helping Arn cross to the Dragn's side. If the Dragn exploded now, all of them would be instantly killed. Of course, the whole of Senedu would die, too, as support arches crumbled, and thousands of tonnes of rock thundered down, corridors buckled, chambers split . . .

No! Gen couldn't think of that now.

"General, you must be careful. A single error and the missile will explode at once," the Wizard said. "But also, you cannot delay."

"I understand."

"You have been born to do this," the Wizard added.

It was like the game, Gen realized — the enormous memory game his father had taught him long, long ago — the Guardian game — the only game the Guardian had ever played with his son. It required complete concentration, absolute accuracy, a flawless memory, no errors allowed. "And no feelings!" the Guardian had said. "The player of this game must have no feelings!"

Occasionally Gen had wondered why no one else in Senedu ever played it.

"Enter the codes now," the Wizard said.

Gen pushed a bewildering series of buttons with his fingers, every bit of his strength concentrated in that one act. He did not think of his own safety, standing dizzy heights above the floor. He did not think of the consequences if he should fail. He felt neither fear nor anger. He lived completely for each letter, each number, his mind a weapon such as the Elders might have used. Lights flashed on and off. Gen was not distracted.

When it was over, Gen found that his hands were trembling. The codes had stopped the missile, Gen thought. He was limp with relief.

"That's it, then. It's done. Can I climb down now?"

Gen had become comfortable with the Wizard's voice, though he had yet to see him. He felt almost as if he spoke to a friend. The icy voice of the missile shattered Gen's nerves. "Time limit exceeded. Countdown resuming. Twenty-eight."

"What is — ? Shouldn't it — ?"

There was a dreadful pause. Then the Wizard spoke. "There is something wrong. The sound of the missile's voice should have stopped. Read off the codes to me again, General."

"Ft764xmfg8fhd8roghe7394hjg8fhdlg8t49s dgs-0gj45dshdt-3ufgk-3yfl0 — Bravo One."

"There is no error in your work, General. The error must be in the Dragn's circuits. They have been damaged by acid leakage from the surface.

We cannot deactivate the Dragn."

"Then what — ?"

Gen felt suddenly sick. Death for all of Senedu! After all they had done to prevent it! Was it unavoidable?

"We must launch the Dragn. No, do not come down yet, General. You must reset the co-ordinates. We will not fire the missile at an enemy. I will calculate a path to send it into outer space, where the poisons it carries will be harmless."

"Twenty-seven."

No! Don't listen to the footsteps of death coming closer! Gen thought for an instant — I can't. I am too afraid!

"Twenty-six."

The Wizard recited a new set of letters and numbers. Gen bent again over the missile panel. Sweat dripped into his eyes. He wiped it away impatiently. You have no choice, he told himself angrily. Your feelings do not matter!

"Launch sequence initiated," the Dragn's vast, echoing voice suddenly announced. "Clear launch area for final countdown. Twenty-five."

"General, you have completed your task. Senedu is safe now. But you must leave this chamber at once or you will be consumed in the fire of the Dragn as it takes flight. Take shelter in the far room, with me. It has special protection."

Gen raced for the floor of the cavern. Below him, Duff shouted.

"Hurry, Gen!"

How could any ladder be so long?

"Eighteen."

To Gen it seemed as if his legs had lost their bones and sagged uselessly below him. His toes fumbled at the rungs, his eyes were full of salt. Climbing down seemed more difficult than climbing up had been.

"Seventeen."

"You can make it, Gen!" Arn said tightly. "Climb!"

Gen's breath rasped in his throat. His hands slipped awkwardly from the handholds, almost useless. Under strain too long, the small muscles of his hands had begun to twitch.

"Fifteen."

"Take shelter in the room marked by the flashing light," the Wizard said. "General, please hurry."

"Thirteen."

Gen looked down. The others huddled at the base of the Dragn, uncertain. Arn, Nirrin, Jered and Duff.

"Run!" Gen called. "Get to safety!"

Arn tried to pull Nirrin away.

"No! We aren't leaving Gen."

"Don't stop climbing, Gen!" Duff called.

"Leave me." Gen's voice failed. He stumbled on the next rung and nearly fell. It was still a long way to the cavern floor.

"Eleven."

"That's it, Gen. Jump!"

Gen glanced below. Jered and Duff held out their arms. "No. I'll hurt you."

"Would you stop being such a weed-head!" Jered shouted. "Or don't you trust us?"

Gen almost smiled. He closed his eyes. He let the rungs slide through his hands, and plummeted to the floor. Jered and Duff broke his fall. The three boys collapsed in a heap at the base of the missile. Precious minims passed as they untangled themselves and stood.

"Five."

Then they ran toward the blinking light. It was so far away! Jered half-carried Arn, and Duff had Gen's arm over one shoulder.

"Three."

They burst into a multi-coloured room. A door unlike anything Gen had ever seen slid shut behind them.

"Two. One. Launch."

Deafening thunder slapped Gen to the floor, struck him like a monstrous hand. The beast that was a machine roared as if centuries of pain and rage erupted from a broken mind. Beneath Gen, the floor bucked and trembled. Stone groaned. Gen's heart stopped. Too late, Gen thought. We waited too long, and death has come. The Dragn will have its prey.

Gen tensed, ready for walls and ceiling to

disintegrate. For a crushing weight to snatch away life and breath. Instead, the thunder doubled, went ravening along Gen's nerves to burst in his mind. The Wizard's chamber shuddered. Then, incredibly, the Dragn's roar diminished. The floor steadied. Rapidly the sound of the Dragn faded. A ringing silence remained.

"Missile Number Four successfully launched," the Wizard said.

"It's over?" Gen breathed. The sound of his own voice was thin in his aching ears.

"It is over. The Dragn is now far away. You have saved Senedu."

The Dragn has flown, Gen thought, and I did not see it. An instant of regret rose up inside Gen. Something terrible, something beautiful and deadly and wondrous was gone. Senedu's enemy was gone. Then overwhelming relief washed over Gen. Death had departed. And Senedu still lived.

Senedu . . . it began to sink in.

"We've done it!"

Gen turned to the others. He grabbed Jered in an awkward hug. He punched Nirrin's shoulder. Suddenly everyone was laughing and talking at once.

"I can hardly believe it!"

"What a day!"

"You can come back with us, Wizard," Gen said. "You don't have to be alone anymore. When we tell my father what you've done for Senedu . . . "

Gen looked up, searching for a body matching the voice he had come to trust. He saw a wall covered with blinking lights and glass windows and mysterious controls. At the top of the wall was one word — Wizard.

Amazed comprehension filled Gen.

Chapter 23

Gen stood motionless before the enormous array of lights, glass windows and buttons. "You — you are the Wizard?" he asked.

"Yes," the Wizard's voice replied. "You see now why I cannot come with you."

"I don't see him," Jered growled. "He's still hiding from us!"

"No." Gen shook his head. "The Wizard never hid from us. He cannot leave this room. Isn't that true?"

"Yes." Was there regret in the Wizard's voice?

"Why not?" Jered asked. "Where is he?"

Gen indicated the large panel. "The Wizard cannot walk. He has no legs. His voice and his awareness carry a long way, but he is not a man. This machine is the Wizard."

"That is so."

"What?"

"I knew I was right!" Duff cried. "I told you not to trust this — creature. He isn't like us. He isn't even human! That old man we saw — "

"Was an image, a picture of the old man who made me. You demanded to see me. I could not meet you in any other way."

"In some ways you were right, Duff. The Wizard is different from us — but that doesn't make him evil. We are different from the other People of Senedu. We need to explore new things. Does that make us evil? No. Remember the Wizard's story? The Elders did not wish to remember that they made the Dragns, that they killed other men. So they blamed the Wizard. But the Wizard was only a servant. And they made him, too."

Gen turned to the panel, waiting to see if his wild guesses were true.

"You are well-suited to your name, General." There was a lightness to the Wizard's voice that was almost like laughter. But it was not laughter. "You have a wisdom beyond your years. You have been well trained."

"Of course," Arn said. "A machine as great as the Dragn."

"Greater," said the Wizard. "The Dragns could never think."

"Still, this isn't a real person," Jered said.

"He may not have been born like us, but he is real," Gen said. "And he is a friend."

"At any rate, we can go home!" Duff said.

Gen turned to grin at his friend.

"Yes."

At last Gen's father would respect him! Gen had done something really important. He had proven himself. He had put the Good of Senedu first, as the Guardian had taught him. Gen saw his father's face in his mind's eye. He saw the granite countenance melt into a smile. He saw himself in his father's embrace.

Finally it would happen. Gen's father would love him.

Arn coughed. "Gen, there's something I must tell you. Your father made you, all of you . . . outcasts."

Gen froze with the smile still on his face.

"Outcasts!" Jered barked. "That mucking, stubborn — "

He caught the look in Gen's eyes and fell silent. Nirrin's face was dark. Duff's was ashen.

"You must be mistaken," Gen said tightly.

Arn shook his head slightly. "I don't know why, but I was there when he began the ritual. Of course, the ritual requires that you receive sentence face to face. The final words have yet to be spoken — "

A strained smile spread across Gen's face. "And they won't be spoken! My father did not understand! When he knows the truth, he won't reject me. He won't reject any of us. We deserve

thanks, not punishment. We just saved the city."
The smile broadened. "My father is the Guardian
of Truth. He can't help but welcome a new truth!
Come on! Let's give him the good news. After all,
we're heroes!"

Gen swept the others along in the force of his
determination. They hurried toward Senedu.

"And I won't leave out your part," Gen called
to the Wizard. "We'll repair these corridors, come
back to live with you. You're Senedu's best
friend!"

Chapter 24

The Wand made it possible for Gen to open the door to Senedu.

His father the Guardian was waiting for them. The rest of the Council stood a little apart, watching.

Gen sprang forward with a smile.

"Father, we saved Senedu! I can't wait to tell you about it!"

The Guardian turned to Arn, as if the children did not exist. He spoke in a low voice that the Council could not hear.

"My brother, I have delayed casting you out, but I cannot delay much longer."

"I understand," Arn said gravely.

"Father! I'm here. I'm alive. Don't you care?" Gen's low voice held years of pain. "I know I displeased you by going into the air tunnels, but if you will only listen, I can make you understand why I did it. We found a Dragn, you see — "

"You were successful in launching the last Dragn?" The Guardian asked Arn. "We heard the thunder of its passing."

"Someone-who-has-no-name was successful, yes."

A spasm crossed the Guardian's face. "I am glad."

Gen caught his breath. "You knew!" he said. "Father, you knew about the Dragn all the time. You knew the truth! How could you have deceived me and all of the People for so long? You even punished me — "

The Guardian's face was stone-still. "It is the Guardian's role to guard the Truth, and sometimes to protect the People from it, my brother." He pretended to speak to Arn, but his words were meant for Gen. Custom made it impossible to speak directly to an outcast. The Council could not hear what the Guardian said, but it watched him carefully.

"Why?" Arn asked, voicing Gen's question.

"Men and women were not made for the caverns, as you were taught. They were made for great open spaces. How could they bear the strong discipline needed for cavern life if they knew the truth? If they had the guilt of war and destruction on their heads — destruction of their entire world, as well as their fellow men? And if they knew there was another world, however poisonous, beyond Senedu?"

"You're wrong, father! The People deserve to know the truth! The world outside is not poisonous anymore. They must know about it. They could live better — "

"Knowing they betrayed other men?" Still the Guardian looked only at his brother. "Knowing they killed millions of innocent people?" The Guardian's rough words cut across Gen's objections.

"We don't have to live here anymore. We could leave the caverns!" Gen cried. "Live in freedom!"

"The People of Senedu do not wish to leave. They are accustomed to life in the caverns. They do not know how to change. Most of them would go mad if they tried. Generation after generation, the People have diminished to suit the caverns. It is too late! And what is freedom without order? Even if they knew about the other world, the People would choose to stay."

"No!" Gen insisted. "If you are so sure of yourself, tell them! Let the People choose for themselves."

For an instant the Guardian's rigid control seemed to crumble. "My son is a fool!" he hissed, stopping himself only with great difficulty from turning to face Gen. "What would you — any of you — offer the People to replace the safety of Senedu? A wild, untamed world where survival must be wrenched from the jaws of savage weather and animals! Danger, violent death, unknown risks. There are no warm sleeping chambers in that world. There are no irrigation pipes or light-lenses."

Gen fell silent for a minim, unsure. What did he really know of the outside? Only what the Wizard had told him while he waited for the key.

"If you tell the People, you rob them of contentment here," the Guardian continued. "And my son cannot pretend that a raw world, where nothing has been built or planted, can give them real hope!"

Gen's face was bitter. "I always thought if we could only talk, if I could explain . . ." he choked. "The new world gives *me* hope, father. Can't you understand? Why did you deny us that?"

Certain Council members stepped forward, suspicious of the delay.

Unspoken words crowded into the Guardian's eyes. A few of them found their way to his lips. "I tried to find the Dragn in my youth," he said quietly, still addressing his brother. "I failed. The time had not yet come."

Behind the Guardian the rest of the Council moved closer. They were becoming impatient. Beyond them, a few hesitant People had begun to gather. Why can't they go away? Gen thought with desperation. Why can't they let my father be simply a father? I need —

"Arn, I understand you have no son," the Guardian said.

"Father!" Gen rasped.

"Not of the body, Guardian," Arn replied. "Though I have one son of the heart."

The Guardian nodded sternly. "My own son is dead. But I could wish you nothing better than to have such a fine boy for your son. A boy who proved his training."

"Thank you, Guardian," Arn said formally.

Gen's eyes blurred. It can't end like this, he longed to shout. I'm not dead. I'm not! Here — look at me — a living boy. Your son!

"Please — "

The Guardian's granite face shifted for a single moment. A look of profound sorrow entered it and was instantly gone. Duty — always duty came first. This man is not my father, Gen thought, he is the Guardian. I have no father. An emptiness almost too painful to bear entered Gen's chest. He saw the Guardian open his mouth and speak the final words of the ceremony to outcast all of them. He did not hear the words. A rushing seemed to fill his ears.

I have no father, Gen thought. And now I have no home. But I have hope.

When the ritual was over, Gen touched a part of the wall with the Wand of Authority.

I am outcast, Gen thought, but I still have a voice. And the People of Senedu will have their choice.

Gen began to speak. According to the law, no one would notice his words. He had no name. He was not of the People. But, ironically, no one could stop him. The Wand activated a system. Gen's words carried to every room in the city.

"People of Senedu, I have a new Truth to tell you. Listen." Through all the corridors of Senedu, Gen's voice echoed. Bakers, farmers, builders, toolmakers, miners, teachers, wardens and children stopped working, turned to the resonant voice that seemed to come from the very walls.

"In the beginning were men and women like us, though we have called them Elders. They made many marvellous things, and they also made terrible things. They were not evil, they were not good — they were people who sometimes made very great mistakes.

"They quarrelled. They made tools to kill each other. These tools they called Dragns. They made a wonderful machine to help send the Dragns on their way. This they called the Wizard. The Wizard was no more evil or good than the men it served. The Dragns were tools — like hammers, with no will of their own.

"Men and women made Senedu as a safe place to hide during the quarrels. Much was destroyed during the quarrels, which were called wars. It was not safe to leave Senedu for a long time.

"Now the quarrels are over. We do not need

to hide anymore. The Sky place is clean and good. Not without dangers — like long-legs, only different. But it is also beautiful. There, farms can be made that need no lenses. There, water flows without irrigation pipes. There, some foods grow without planting, in fields that have no end. There the ceiling is very far away.

"I and my friends will go to the Sky place and make a life there. It will be hard work and Senedu will not take us back once we have gone.

"At the end of the Long Corridor I will wait one watch. Then I will go forever. If anyone wishes to join me, come now.

"I am Gen."

Gen stopped speaking. He had never made such a speech before.

Chapter 25

The People of Senedu approached the end of the Long Corridor. Gen waited for them there. Some carried sacks of seeds, clothing, tools and food. Hamar, the farmer, and his family; Illys and her other sons — stout men; Quig, masterbuilder, and a handful of his apprentices; Sarin, with a hand loom; and more young men with restless eyes, women with bundles of herbs, and lumps of bread yeast, and clay bowls, and blankets. At the fringes of the group were many who looked uncertainly at the Guardian.

The Guardian raised his voice. "Illys is dead . . . "

The Guardian began the ceremony that would outcast all who passed the door of Senedu. There would be no returning if the Sky place proved to be harsh and inhospitable. This was clear. A few of the People who had brought sacks quietly faded into the back of the crowd and disappeared, returning to their tasks. But most of the People who had gathered set their faces and walked past the Guardian.

Isolated groups watched sadly as the outcasts disappeared beyond the door. The Guardian stepped forward.

"It is time for the Long Corridor to be sealed." The Guardian spoke as if to the air. For he could speak to none of the outcasts again.

Gen handed the Wand to his father. The Guardian pretended not to see. Gen laid the Wand on the floor and his father stooped to pick it up.

A whisper passed the Guardian's lips — the fragment of another ceremony. "May the dead find happiness in the afterlife."

Then the Guardian straightened.

It would be a better life than the life of the outcast — of that Gen was sure. Anything would be better than that. Why, then, was it so hard to leave Senedu, and this man?

"Goodbye," Gen whispered, though the dead cannot say goodbye.

The Guardian passed the Wand over the centre of the door frame. The panel slid shut.

To those who watched the Guardian seal the door, it seemed that he had suddenly become an old man.

Chapter 26

The lamp-lighters were stirring. The duties of the day were about to begin. The Guardian rose from the chair in which he had spent the night. He moved stiffly.

So it was done. The migration predicted by every Guardian since the beginning had taken place at last. Or had it just begun?

I have done well, the Guardian told himself. I prepared my son perfectly, so that he would test the limits and find if the time was right. I gave him strength, the hardness needed in a General. I made him train his hands, so that his fingers would not falter when they held the lives of the People. I gave him a stubborn, searching spirit. I gave him discontentment. I did what I had sworn, as a General, to do.

The right time came. Gen found what I could not find. He met the challenge.

I withdrew the guards and wardens from these passages, I left the Wand of Authority where it could be found, I did all that I could do to help my son find the Truth. And after he had found it, I tested him with words. If he had not been the chosen one, he would have turned back.

Were your words only a test? the Guardian asked himself. Or did you believe them? You did not want Gen to leave. You will never see your son again, never be able to take away the accusation in his eyes . . .

The Guardian shook his head, suppressing his wandering thoughts.

The New World has come, he told himself. My son leads the courageous ones into the future. I have done well.

Why, then, do I feel so empty?

The Guardian plunged his face into a washbasin, changed his clothes, readied himself for the first tasks of the day.

About seventy of the People had gone with Gen to start new lives. The Guardian hoped the Vandals and other malcontents were among them. Senedu would be that much more at peace. Still, others would have to take up their tasks. A thousand details and adjustments awaited the Guardian's attention.

The rest of the People would stay in Senedu, at least until the next generation. They needed the close, comforting walls of the caverns. They needed the Rules and the Guardian. They would forget Gen's words because they wanted to forget. They would return to the old Truth. The discipline that the Guardian had maintained would be their refuge. The Truths he had given so much to protect would comfort them.

Why does this give me no joy? the Guardian asked himself.

The answer was unimportant. Feelings did not matter. Duty, the Good of Senedu — that was what mattered. But a fleeting, errant thought betrayed the Guardian as he turned to meet the door warden.

At least my son is free.

Chapter 27

The ceiling was blue and so far above Gen's head that he could not touch it. Yellow light poured from a place in the ceiling too bright to look at. Where the light touched Gen's skin, he felt warm.

There were no walls, no walls anywhere. I can run, Gen thought, without stopping to turn corners. But not yet. Now, he stood enraptured by the scene before him. The people behind crowded forward with cries of delight.

A great pool of water glistened deep blue ahead. Plants of awesome height marched into the distance. Lush green fields surrounded the waters. New words, Gen thought. We will have to learn new words for this beauty. The Wizard will help us.

Snatches of sentences came to Gen's ears.

"But it's so big!"

"So alive!"

Yes, that was the word! Everywhere Gen looked, living things crowded one another. Splashes of yellow and red touched the field with warmth. Gen had never seen so many colours. His head reeled. And the smells! Sweet, sharp, rich odours vied for Gen's attention. He breathed deeply. A soft hand seemed to brush against Gen's face. The air was moving, without tunnels! Leaves rustled with a sound like music.

Was this the raw, untamed world that the Guardian had feared? Gen had never seen such loveliness or felt such freedom. Awe and excitement flooded through him. What was beyond those tall plants? Gen couldn't wait to find out! He knew it would be something new. This was a new world to explore. What could be better? A world free of the suffocating regulations and duties of Senedu! A world where walls didn't hem you in.

You will never go home again, a truant voice inside Gen whispered.

I am home, Gen answered it. And for the first time in his life, he knew it to be true.

Jered came up beside Gen. "So what's the plan?"

Gen frowned. "Do you have a plan?"

"Well, no. But . . . "

"Then why do you expect me to have one?"

Jered's eyes widened. "Why, because you're Guardian!"

Nirrin chuckled as she joined them. "Someone has to lead."

"Despite your lack of sense . . . " Duff added with a grin.

No, Gen thought. That isn't what I want of a new world! "We can discuss our plans together," he said stubbornly.

"Of course," Nirrin agreed.

"We can vote."

"Yes." His cousin smiled. "And then you can tell us what to do."

The entire group came to a halt as Gen paused. They waited to see what he would do next.

"You are extremely irritating, Nirrin!" Gen snapped. "You always have been! And how can you agree with them, Duff? As for you, Jered — !"

From a few paces away, Gen saw Arn watching. There was an understanding smile on the man's face.

All these people have followed me into an unknown world, Gen thought. And I haven't the faintest idea what to do next.

Gen looked at the faces of the people. He saw wonder, joy, fear. Some held their hands over their heads, frightened of the vast size of the sky. But most were smiling. No, not just smiling — intoxicated with the lush, green beauty of this new place.

Behind them, Gen saw a tree laden with

some kind of fruit. And in that field — wasn't that grain growing?

Since Gen had stopped talking, Jered and Nirrin had started to fight.

"First, we should make some shelters for the dark watches," Jered suggested.

"No, first we should explore the nearest food sources."

"Hah! A typical girl's attitude!"

"If you insult me once more — !"

Gen shook his head. A huge, warm grin spread over his face. He raised his voice so it would carry above the argument. "Welcome to the new world," Gen said.

And for the very joy of it, he could not help laughing.